# The Writers @ Lovedean

www.thewriterslovedean.co.uk

978-1-4466-5923-6

# Acknowledgements

As always, I am very grateful
to all the people who made this book possible:
Lynne, Barbara, Helen, Pat, Carol and Toni
for their endless editing and in some cases
the use of their dining rooms.

Thanks to Lynne our
unofficial treasurer who was willing to
hide our cash in her knickers drawer.

Bryan and Graham for the willingness to
sell inflatable blow up clown suits to raise
funds.

And also to the 'friends of The Writers@Lovedean'
who despite having no inclination to put pen to
paper themselves have helped the group.
Yvonne, Simon and Brian

Lastly I would like to thank my
wonderful husband, Simon, for formatting
and uploading our work

# Contents

# Works by Lynne Stone

# Father by Coincidence

"Mum, talk to me." James looked at his Mother. Her thin frame hunched over the kitchen table.

"There is nothing to say James. You are leaving tomorrow for University and life will change for both of us, for five years," said Maggie looking at her beloved son who had turned eighteen the week before.

"Mum, you promised." he said.

"James it will do no good at all to rake over the past. Go away, fulfill your dream and have a good time and forget the past." answered Maggie.

"That's not fair. You always said when I was old enough; you would tell me about my father. All I know is you gave me his name."

Maggie sighed, and looked at her son. "James make me a cup of tea and I'll tell you. I can't bear the thought of you going away with bad feeling between us, but I warn you there is very little to tell."

James put the mug down in front of his mother. She looked older than her thirty five years and he felt sorry for her. She had worked hard to give him everything, but in doing so she had lost herself. She was just a single mum, without a social life and soon to be alone.

"Ok mum, tell me." said James quietly.

"Your father, Barry Rawlings was the only man I ever loved." Maggie hesitated her voice cracking with emotion. "We were at school together and inseparable but our parents did everything to keep us apart. Then one night Barry came round and broke the terrible news his families were moving to Australia and he had to go. We were both seventeen, and scared. We slept together just the once, the night before he sailed to Australia."

"So does he know about me?" he asked quietly.

"I think so," whispered Maggie.

"What do you mean, you think so?" questioned James.

"I did write and tell him I was pregnant and he promised to come back as soon as he could. Then the letters dried up and I haven't heard anything for years," said Maggie a tear running down her face.

"Have you never tried to find him Mum?" asked James.

"No James. I couldn't face it. My parents threw me out and I had to make a life for us and I always thought if he really loved me he would have come back." Maggie looked at her sons face. "I'm sorry James but that is all there is, I have done everything I can to be a Mum and a Dad for you."

"Am I like him Mum?" asked James.

"Oh James yes, even now every time I look at you, I'm reminded of your father," Maggie replied.

"A photo. Do you have a photo Mum?" asked James.

Maggie hesitated, "Well I just have one, but even now it pains me to look at it."

"Can I see it please Mum?"

Maggie stood up and walked over to the dresser and got out an old biscuit tin "this is the only photo, I have." she handed a torn photo of a young man to James.

"Whatever happened to the other half Mum?"

"Well James, it was the only photo we had of each other and we didn't have the technology you have today so we just tore it in half, and Barry took a picture of a young and happy me with him to Australia."

James watched as his mother placed the photo back in the biscuit tin and said, "So there is nothing else you can tell me about my Father. Do you know where he is now?"

"No there is nothing more to tell and I have no idea where he is now." Maggie paused and looking at her sons anxious face said, "It was not the way I had planned my life but honestly I wouldn't have done anything any differently." said Maggie.

"Mum, you've been brilliant but now you really need to get a life. You never go out; you never have fun, promise me that you will try to build a new life while I'm away."

"James, I'm happy as I am and I'm so proud of you going to Oxford to study Medicine."

"Mum you're still young, have some fun." said James.

James was due to leave for University a week later but determined that he would not let the subject of his father drop he waited until his mother was out and he retrieved the photo from the tin and scanned it in to his laptop. At some point later he would do something about finding his father, but right now he was more worried about leaving his fragile Mother alone.

Once at Oxford James relaxed and didn't think too hard about finding his father, sure he went on to Facebook and Friends Reunited but Barry Rawlings remained elusive and he had a new life and a mountain of studying to do.

James was an avid reader and with some like minded friends he registered in Book Crossing, after reading that there were some785, 000 members, and it was fascinating tracking the global movement of the books. He registered six books including his all time favorite "The Hobbit" by Tolkien ,and at the last minute inside each one he put a copy of the photo of his father, his own name and mobile phone number simply asking do you know this man?

James did track the books for a while but soon lost interest as life at Oxford took over.

So a few months later when he logged on to the website he was surprised to find that all of his books had gone abroad. The Hobbit was in Adelaide airport. One had turned up in a bar in Portugal and the others appeared to be travelling around Europe.

A few weeks later James took a call on his mobile.

"Hi, this is Barry Rawlings; I picked up a book of yours at Adelaide airport."

James was silent for a moment then he spoke. "How do I know you are really Barry Rawlings?"

"Well James, we need to meet up and you can judge for yourself." said Barry.

James took a deep breathe and said "Yes lets do that, where are you?"

"I'm in London where you are?"

"I'm in Oxford." answered James.

"I can catch a train and be in Oxford tomorrow," said Barry decisively.

James was almost speechless and said, "OK ring me when you arrive and I will meet you."

With that he hung up his hands shaking. This had to be a hoax; he couldn't have found his real Dad could he?

James hardly slept that night. All he could see was his worn out mother and the torn photo of his father. Morning came and James couldn't eat. He drank endless cups of black coffee and then the phone rang. "Hi James its Barry. I'm in the garden of a pub called The Trout the taxi driver dropped me here saying it's popular with students,. Do you know it?"

"Sure it's just a short walk away from my campus, see you in ten minutes." said James.

James paused only long enough to pick up his keys and walked down the road to The Trout which was his local watering hole. His pace slowed as he approached, he took a deep breath. What if this was a hoax?

The garden, that's where Barry said he would be, James walked round the back, picked up a pint at the bar and looked around. The garden was quiet but there was no mistaking Barry Rawlings. Instinctively James knew now exactly how he would look in seventeen years time.

James walked over to Barry and shook his hand. "Hello son." he said quietly

James replied, "It's a bit soon for that isn't it?"

Barry put his hand into his jacket pocket and put onto the table the other half of the photo that James had never seen. His mum, young and very obviously in love with this man Barry, his dad, if his mum was speaking the truth, and one look told him it was the truth.

James looked at the photo and struggled to hold back the tears, and then he spoke "I think this is proof but this is all very hard for me to take in. I have so many questions; I really don't know where to start"

"I understand," said Barry gently. "Why don't I just tell you about what happened and you can judge for yourself?"

"No wait, first tell me why did you pick up the book?" asked James.

"The Hobbit is my favourite book of all time. I read it when I was fourteen and loved it and I have always meant to read it again. There it was on the bench at the airport while I was waiting for my flight and I couldn't resist picking it up."

"Amazing," said James, "Now what about my Mum?"

Barry took a sip of his pint and began. "I was in love with your mother, but our families didn't approve, my Mum and Dad immigrated to Australia and being only seventeen I had to go with them. I always intended to come back, I knew Maggie was pregnant, but she stopped writing and I never knew if I was a father or not. I went through University and trained as a Doctor. I did make a couple of attempts to contact Maggie but she never answered my letters. Time went on and when I was offered a job here in London. I decided to take the job and at the same time make a concerted effort to meet up again with Maggie." He hesitated and went on, "When I picked up the book at Adelaide airport I was about to put it into my suitcase when the picture of me fell out. To say I was astounded is an understatement. All at once I realised I did have a child, a son and he wanted to find me. I rang you as soon as I got off the plane at Heathrow."

"I really don't know what to say," said James hesitantly. "For me there is a lot to think about and Mum, well she never married and she has been a brilliant Mother. I really don't know how she will react." he stopped mid sentence and then asked "What about you Barry? Did you marry?"

"No, I never met anyone who measured up to your mother, please don't speak to her, tell me where she lives now and I will surprise her." said Barry.

"Oh she will be surprised alright," said James as he handed over his home address. "Barry you will find her there. She never goes far from home."

Barry stood up and said, "I think we both need some time to adjust. Right now I want to meet up with your mum and see if we have a future together, but we will keep in contact and hopefully we can build a relationship."

James shook Barry's hand and watched as his Father walked away. Everything seemed right and James felt sure after just one meeting that he had at last looked in to the eyes of the man that he would eventually become.

## Goodbye, Hello

Rodney stood on the platform surrounded by crying children clinging to their mother's skirts. Only he wasn't crying he was smiling. His mother had left him at the station an hour early. Her lunch with his latest Uncle was more important than seeing her only son leave London for the country. She leant forward to kiss him but she pulled away from his rigid figure saying 'Bye Roddy, see you when this wretched war is over.' And she strode away without looking back.

Rodney had sighed with relief as he watched her turn the corner. He was an only child his mother left him alone daily, now he was going to have an adventure. The vicar's wife checked their labels and herded them on to the train. Rodney sat in a corner heart pounding with anticipation, he hadn't slept well lately and the rhythm of the train soon had him asleep.

Three hours later the train pulled into the station. Rodney rubbed his eyes and looked out at the unfamiliar countryside, the platform full of families waiting for all the evacuees. He stood in line as the vicar's wife called them one by one, and then he heard it, 'Rodney Morton.'

Tentatively he looked up, a plump rosy faced woman held out her hand saying 'Hello Rodney call me Mum, and these are your new brothers.' She clasped him to her ample bosom a broad beam appeared on his face with tears coursing down his cheek, he whispered 'Hello Mum.'

# Land of Opportunity

It had taken him months to get this far. His bare feet were calloused and sore where his oversized shoes had rubbed him raw, forcing him to abandon them at the roadside somewhere between Germany and France.

Born in Romania to a family of travelers, Beryx had spent most of his childhood travelling round Poland. He was friends with Aleksy a Polish boy. The pair were inseparable and spent hours planning to leave Poland for a better life in England.

They didn't go to school but spent a few hours' fruit picking to get some money together. It was when Beryx overheard his parents saying it was time to move on, that Alexys said, "We have to go now, your family are going back to Romania. Mine are staying here, we will be miles apart and if we don't go now we won't ever go."

"But we have hardly any money saved," said Beryx.

"Well we're going to have to do it the best we can and if necessary beg and borrow our way across Europe," answered Aleksy matter of fatly.

"England is a long way from here," said Beryx stating the obvious.

"Well that's our choice either we sit here dreaming or we start walking and look out for rides," said Aleksy with conviction.

"Yes I suppose you are right," said Beryx.

The pair sneaked out very early one morning carrying their possessions in small rucksacks. The first few days were tough but they walked and hitch hiked always getting dropped off in towns so they could go through the bins for scraps of food and where they could, use washrooms in cafes to have a wash. The days turned in to weeks and Beryx's enthusiasm grew but Aleksy missed his family he gave up at the German border when he saw the armed Policja.

"Sorry Beryx I am scared and want to go back, come with me?"

"No Aleksy I have come this far and I know it's a long hard road, but I have nothing to go back for, I am carrying on."

Aleksy shrugged and said "I'm sorry."

"Good luck I will miss you." said Beryx and Alexy watched him walk without looking back.

Beryx walked on a little then sat on the side of the road holding his rucksack, the customs barrier in front of him. The border was very busy, a constant stream of traffic but without a passport it was going to be very difficult, to get through.

It was a warm night so Beryx decided to walk back a bit out of sight and rest. He found a ditch and lay down and was very soon asleep.

He woke up hours later to the sound of birdsong cold and covered in dew and looked around him, he now had to concentrate on getting across the border.

He sat looking for a couple of hours, and decided to walk back further , he had watched and very few officers bothered to lift the covers on the lorries so he would take a chance and sneak on to the next  lorry that slowed down by him. Beryx didn't have to wait long; he stood up and ran behind the lorry grabbing at the back as it reduced speed. He slid under the canvas cover and squeezed into a space between a couple of large pieces of machinery.

The lorry moved on and there was lots of shouting but it was in Polish and Beryx lay waiting to be discovered.

But then the lorry began moving faster and he reckoned that for some time he could ignore his hunger, ignore his craving for food and thirst and just sleep and sleep he did.

Hours later the lorry juddered to a halt and Beryx peeped out, it had stopped at a service station

Time to jump out and he went to the gents and locked himself in to a cubicle.  He was alone so had a quick wash and took a long swig of water straight from the tap. He needed food, he walked out on to the forecourt, and his "ride" had gone. Beryx's heart sank. What now?

He walked across the road the soles of his boots flapping. He sat down, and took off his boots and tossed them to one side, and watched the service station.

Cars and lorries were pulling in all the time to buy fuel and food. Beryx couldn't remember the last time he had eaten. After a short while one of the picnic benches was empty and the family drove off leaving the remains of their supper there. Casually he walked over and sat at the bench, and began to eat greedily. He decided to sleep under a bench. He walked to the toilet and filled a discarded bottle with water and then settled down for the night.

Beryx woke in the morning as the sun came up. He had to get moving today, all he knew was that he was still in Germany and had a long way to go.

Refreshed, he walked a few yards back from the service station, waiting for an opportunity, and soon enough it came. A truck pulled in and the driver locked the cab and went in to the café for breakfast. Beryx saw his chance his water bottle was full and he had been through the bins and had found discarded food he could manage for a few days on this. Beryx decided to take a risk, he had no idea where this truck was going but he was taking no chances he was going to get under the cover and go with it. This time he wouldn't get out at a service station and lose his ride, he would stay on board until the end, wherever that would be.

Beryx lifted the cover and crawled into a space, his thin frame fitting between two crates. The truck began to move, but the motion and the fumes meant that Beryx was unaware most of the time of where he was and what was going on. He was aware that they had arrived in France, and surprised that not once had the cover been lifted. He didn't know how long he had been confined to this small space, he knew he stank but he had made it this far and he wasn't going to give up until there was no choice.

The truck shuddered to a halt a few times in France, but Beryx just sneaked out to relieve himself in the bushes and quickly went through the bins for food always making sure he was back in his hidey hole before the driver was back in the cab.

Eventually the truck pulled into a lay by, and the driver was asleep Beryx could hear his snores. He crept out and looked around him. The sign said Cherbourg 70km. He was disorientated, so nearly there, he knew there was very little chance of getting through Cherbourg but it was too late to worry now he was nearly there. Beryx walked about a bit to stretch his legs and sat on the roadside watching the sun come up, sensing that if he sat around much longer he may be caught he crawled back to his space and went immediately to sleep.

Lack of food and drink and the fumes from the truck meant he was very weak and time passed quickly as he drifted in and out of sleep, unaware of most that was going on around him. He peered out and he was relieved he was in the hold of a ship on his way to England. He had slept through the customs in Cherbourg, now he had to stay where he was he didn't want to get caught before they landed in England.

Beryx lay there, Aleksy wouldn't believe him, he had made it, he was in the England -The Land of Opportunity

The truck parked up and he waited until the driver started to snore, he peeped out and it was pitch black he would have to wait until daylight.

Beryx woke as the truck began to move, hungry, thirsty and very disorientated. It's not a problem he thought next time he stops I'm getting out.

A short time later, he hears raised voices his heart is pounding, he's made it,

But now he feels frightened where is he?

Gingerly he lifts the cover, he wriggles his body trying to move his limbs after so long cooped up and with one leap he is out of the truck, he is momentarily disorientated, he hears a shout and he runs, he doesn't get very far before he is surrounded, by armed police. He doesn't understand a word that anyone says to him, but he appears to be in a military naval base, and there is no way out. But he has made it and for him there is no going back. He is at the end of his journey, he is free, and he's made it to the land of opportunity.

## Serena

Serena threw the snowy white tablecloth over the pine table, smoothed it with her perfectly manicured hands. Today she was making lunch for two friends she hadn't seen for 7 years; she so wanted it to be perfect. The weather was unusually warm and sunny so Serena had dragged the table out of the kitchen and into the garden and was setting it under the apple tree. Her garden wasn't very big but the apple tree stood in the far corner and gave a lovely view of her cottage.

She wheeled out her mother's old trolley and began to put the food onto the table. First the tomatoes, still on the vine plucked from her greenhouse only hours ago. Unable to resist Serena lifted the bowl to sniff the tantalizing smell of tomato. Next to this she put a bowl of freshly cut lettuce mixed with peppery rocket and her own grown cucumbers,

washed and shiny but not cut, Serena remembered some of the best lunches the three of them had eaten were where the food was fresh and rustic and the cucumber was cut in chunks along with the freshly baked French bread and the home made pate she had lovingly prepared yesterday. Lastly the cheeses she held the ripe Brie and memories washed over her.

Serena sat for a moment her mind back in the South of France, she smiled as she remembered she hadn't wanted to go but Dom had been insistent. He had reasoned and pleaded but it wasn't until he turned up in an old Camper van did she relent, originally they were going to drive down to the South of France to pick grapes, this was during the long summer holiday from University, but Dom hadn't done his homework and the grapes weren't ready for picking . So it had to be plan B and they had ended up at a camp site on the beach not far from St Tropez. Their job was to clean the tents and caravans before the new arrivals came and for this they earned enough to put petrol in the campervan and eat and drink well for the summer they had their own well equipped tent and free time to explore.

Serena had fallen in love with The South of France but out of love with Dom. Luckily they made friends with another couple the same age as them doing much the same and the girls hooked up and the boys spent their spare time philosophizing about the meaning of life and how they weren't ever going to join the nine to five gang in fact all they wanted was earn enough money to spend their days fishing swimming and their evenings drinking copious amounts of rough red wine.

The foursome became two twosomes, Marie and Serena and Brad and Dom, the girls sunbathed and shopped, there was no falling out just lots of laughter and at the end of the season Dom admitted to Serena that he was staying on, Serena smiled and calmly said she was going back and Brad had offered her a lift, it was time to get a job and join the real world. Marie was going to follow them but had her eye on a new lifeguard and was just going to see how things panned out. Dom, well Dom was just going to find himself and wasn't prepared to make any decisions, he would wait and move on when he had to.

Serena had never seen Dom since, occasionally a brief call or a postcard but after the first year these petered out. This hadn't stopped her looking back at those halcyon days and wondering had she made the right decision by coming home and pursuing her dream of being a lawyer or should she have stayed in the South of France with Dom?

Out of the blue last week her heart had double flipped when a letter from Dom had arrived with the news he was married, married to Marie and they wanted to come and visit this week. This had thrown Serena into a complete turmoil; she had been upset that she had lost touch with Marie, now she knew why Marie had never come back to the UK.

She had stayed travelling and Serena realised she must have been with Dom all the time.

She had felt a pang of jealousy shoot through her that could have been her couldn't it?

But no she had chosen the sensible option or so she thought, but she wouldn't know until she saw Dom and Marie again.

Serena smiled to herself she was nervous about meeting up with them again, but at the same time proud of what she had achieved since that summer of 2000. She had a really good life and career now and was not afraid to look back at the past.

She glanced at her watch, time to get the wine out of the fridge and just make sure the spare room looked fresh. Serena's stomach started to churn, what if she found she still had feelings for Dom? After all they had been lovers for 3 years through Uni and she had outgrown him or had she?  And Marie, they had become such good friends, why had she never contacted her? So many questions, too late now the door bell rang leaving Serena in even more of a dither.

She opened the door with a thudding heart and the years slipped away, she was drawn to Dom first, she hugged him and noted happily the receding hairline and paunch but immediately she realised the magic had definitely gone. When had he got so old and so scruffy?

Then Marie, Serena threw her arms around her but was disappointed it was a little like embracing a statue, she shrunk back and said "Marie you look fantastic." So it was a lie only a white one Serena assured herself, but Marie had aged her skin lined from too much sun and smoking too many Gitanes. Her hair was lank and somewhere along the line her sparkle had gone.

Serena led them into the garden hastily dumping their overnight bags in the hall, they sat in the shade under the apple tree and Dom said "Serena you look amazing what is your secret?"

Serena answered "If I am honest I think it's because I am truly happy. I have a great job, good friends and an amazing life" she tailed off as she looked at Dom.

Dom looked taken surprised, "Did you marry Serena."

Serena felt uncomfortable, "Well yes Dom I have been married for 5 years."

"You never told me." Said Dom quietly.

"And you never told me about Marie in fact I didn't know wither Marie was alive or dead." Serena turned to Marie "What happened to you Marie I thought we were friends? But you never made so much as a phone call or sent a postcard."

"We were friends Serena," whispered Marie "But I was upset when Brad didn't want to stay with me in France and once he had come home I realised I really loved him I did call him but he didn't want to know, so I decided just to travel a bit on my own," she hesitated, "I didn't meet up with Dom until last year when we bumped in to each other in Mexico."

"Mexico?" queried Serena.

"Yes Mexico any way we were both lonely and if I'm honest one day after too many Tequilas it seemed like a good idea to get married." Marie replied "After all we were good friends."

"Well congratulations," said Serena, "that's fantastic" she looked at their faces "so what is the problem, you don't look very happy?"

"Oh nothing we don't deserve" said Dom we just knew it was a mistake ten minutes after the ceremony in fact as soon as we sobered up. Anyway we are stopping off here for a month and then we are going to India."

"So you aren't going to settle down properly then?" asked Serena.

"No it's not for me." said Dom.

"What about you Marie?" asked Serena as she poured more wine into their glasses.

"Me oh suppose I am going to India, with Dom if we don't get on I will move on."

"But you have a degree in Law why don't you use it?" asked Serena.

"I just can't see myself living in the UK, I have been away too long." said Marie.

"Marie we have choices and as long as you make the right choice in life and it makes you happy, then that's fine we should never have regrets." Serena looked directly at Dom as she spoke, confident that these so called friends had made the wrong decisions in life and she had made the right ones.

Serena stood up and said I have a couple of little surprises for you , my husband will be home any minute" As she spoke the back gate swung open Serena smiled "Marie, Dom I believe you remember Brad ?" she paused as their twins ran across the garden to their Mother.

"These little monsters are Millie and Giles." she said proudly.

Marie and Dom looked at the scene in front of them and their faces fell as Brad walked towards his wife and put his arm around her waist and said "It is so good to see you two again, it's been a long time, and I believe congratulations are in order."

# The Day

The sun was just coming up as I left what remains of my house. Every bone in my body ached. I longed for a comfortable bed to sleep in. I dreamed of crisp clean sheets and wanted to curl up in a duvet, but my bed was long gone, burnt to give me some warmth during the long bitterly cold winter months.

I loaded my dirty washing and some empty buckets into a rusty old supermarket trolley. Which I kept chained to a post in the back yard. I set off and pushed the trolley down the street and up the hill. I swear the hill got steeper each week, or was I just getting weaker?

The trolley wasn't heavy but the wheels had a mind of their own. My heart lifted a little as I reached the top of the hill, I can see the stream at the bottom, the water glistening in the early morning sun, just a small stream but water nevertheless. It's easier going downhill but the pessimist in me knows it will be harder walking back. The buckets will be full, making the trolley heavier to push.

The stream is busy even though it's early. I find a spot and fill my buckets first and load them into the trolley. My laundry on the floor. It's a ritual. There is a part of me that believes the water is cleaner earlier in the day and I feel happier drinking it if I know I have washed myself and my clothes after I have filled the buckets. I take off my clothes and walk in to the water, I am always nervous at this point, I look around cautiously - no Strangers, plenty of faces I recognise, we never speak just nod. We have lived in fear for so long no-one speaks, it is enough to know we are alive, conversation died on The Day.

In a short moment I feel safe and clean although a part of me wishes for soap and a fluffy towel to dry my tired body with. I shake my head at the memory. It doesn't do to remember how it was, memories don't help me get through the days and long nights.

The washing done .I spread it out on the grass and lay back to let the sun dry my body and soak into my weary bones.

I must have dozed off as I woke with a start when a deep voice whispered my name. "Mary, Mary wake up you'll get burnt lying in the sun too long."

I opened my eyes and stared at him. "Who are you? How did you know my name? Why are you talking to me? Are you Stranger?"

"No Mary I am not a Stranger. I live near you, I remember you from…"

"Shush we aren't allowed to talk about before," I said.

"I know but the rules are slightly relaxed now and general conversation is allowed. I'm John Balfour and I knew your husband Chris, we worked together. I live in the street behind you I see you on your own. Whatever happened to Chris?" he asked me

I looked up at him and asked him to sit down. I looked around and noticed other people chatting. "I'm sorry John I haven't spoken to anyone for months I'm always too scared, I'm not sure what we are allowed to talk about anymore. But Chris spoke about you often." I said my mouth dry and my voice very croaky. I tried to remember the last time I had spoken and couldn't. Sure I had muttered to myself when alone in my house but conversation no.

John smiled and said "I know, it's been the same for me but regulations have been changed this week. Now we are allowed conversation but we will be imprisoned if we are heard to be talking about The Day."

His smile lit up his face and I realized how lonely I had been without any conversation and how isolated I had been without company for months and only memories to keep me going. I looked at him and said, "If you live near me then you can help me push this trolley back." he laughed and said "Of course but I shall want a cup of tea as payment."

I looked at him and laughingly asked "Earl Grey or Darjeeling?"

John winced and said "I would much prefer nettle if you can manage."

We walked along in companionable silence until John asked quietly. "So what did happen to your Chris?"

I hesitated; it seemed so long ago but still such a painful memory. I realised as he waited for me to answer that I have lived with this memory so long but never spoken the words to anyone. I took a deep breath, I am not sure what it was about John, but I trusted him and I felt I needed to talk after so long in silence.

"The Day?"

John nodded encouraging me to go on.

I went on, "The Day it happened Chris was in the hospital. He was miles away from here and I could only get to see him once a week, I had been the day before, while there were still buses and he had seemed bright enough." I  paused and John said gently, "Carry on."

"When I left him he was looking forward to coming home but needed to be stronger first, he still needed a machine to help with his breathing." I felt my voice waver. The words hurting as they left my mouth.

"Then it happened. My first thought was to get to Chris; I left my house and walked. I didn't know where I was going, just kept walking and when I eventually got there, there were people everywhere and armed Strangers at the door of the hospital. I begged to be let in, but no-one was allowed in. I slept in the park opposite for a couple of days but as the realisation that the Strangers were now in charge and the air was filled with fear. I left Chris in the hospital."

I paused, now the tears were pouring down my cheeks. John was silent pushing my trolleys, listening to me pour my heart out. I carried on. "I walked home, it took me three days and nights, I had no food or water and I was filled with fear and upset because I felt so helpless and I knew I had left Chris to die."

"It wasn't your fault Mary, the Strangers ruined all our lives, what happened next?" he asked.

"When I got home the street had been barricaded off but I crawled under the barrier and got into my house." I answered.

"Was your house undamaged?" John asked.

"Yes it was. My neighbours had gone and Strangers were guarding the road so looters hadn't got down there, and then the Strangers just moved away and the looters swarmed in."

"How did you survive?" John asked me.

"It was hard, my heart was broken, and I felt my life was over but my survival instincts took over and I protected myself and my property."

"How did you do that?"

"Chris had a gun locked away in a cupboard, I had no key but I broke the lock and waved the gun at anyone who came near me. It wasn't loaded but the looters didn't know that. I also befriended a hungry dog and he drove anyone away from my home. He became my protector so I survived." I paused as the realisation that I had said those words out loud for the first time.

I went on hesitantly "You're the first person I have had a conversation with in all this time." I said looking at his wedding ring.

"It has been tough for all of us Mary, and you did all you could. You couldn't have done any more."

"I know that now but talking to you is making me feel better. Your wife, where is she now?"

John looked uncomfortable, "This isn't easy Mary and I have never told another soul." He paused and went on, "When The Strangers moved in to our street Mary took a shine to one of them and when they moved out she went with them."

"Did she go willingly?" asked Mary quietly.

"To this day I don't know. She was always a flighty piece was Linda, she packed a case and left her wedding ring on the side, so I kind of figured it wasn't kidnap." He paused as Mary looked at him in disbelief.

She said quietly, "One way or another we are all victims now." She paused "Right here we are, I still have a front door, not a lot of furniture, loads of useless electrical equipment"

John laughed "We all have TV's and computers and numerous other electrical devices that we once thought we couldn't live without. Devices that are obsolete now and we don't have any where to dump these, so they sit useless in our homes, just a constant reminder of how it was."

I asked John to come in and I offered to make him nettle tea. He lit the fire for me to boil the water while I picked some nettles from the overgrown back yard.

When I got back inside the water had boiled and John walked towards me and put his arms around me." Mary, life will never be the same again for any of us but we can share our sorrows. We can share our memories, no-one can take that away from us, but we could do it together. We have been alone and living in fear for far too long. The

Strangers allow friendship as long as we don't talk openly about before The Day"

I looked at him and I knew he was right. We could face the future together, whatever it held, it would never be easy but it was better than the isolation we both had now.

# Works by Carol Russell

# Alison Goodwin

Alison Goodwin groaned as she knelt in the church where her family had worshipped for generations. How cold the old building felt in winter, and what a smell of damp there was in the air. Where was her lip balm? She never left the house without it. She fumbled noisily in her huge handbag. How boring the new Vicar's voice sounded. Surely the prayers should have finished by now. As she sat back in the pew she thought how miserable it felt to be getting old.

She gazed about the congregation noting that they were all her age, or more. People she had known all her life. How ancient some of them now appeared. How did she appear to them she wondered idly. Come on, she remonstrated with herself, pay attention to the Vicar. But she found it increasingly difficult to pay attention these days. Her eyes alighted on Mary Newham. A sly smile slowly spread over Alison's face. If only you knew, she thought, you wouldn't be sitting there so pleased with yourself.

At the end of the service she sought out Mary Newham.

"How are you, Mary?" Alison asked, trying desperately to sound sincere in her enquiry.

"Thanks so much for asking, Miss Goodwin, I'm fine. Just off to spend a few days with the grandchildren."

"You lucky person," Alison said wistfully. "I would have loved to have had grandchildren myself."

Alison thought how empty her life had become. She rattled around in the huge farmhouse, alone since her parents had died. Her only visitors were her daily help from the village and the postman. Her sisters and brother hardly ever came to visit, and her nieces and nephews were now grown up with lives of their own. The monthly meeting of the W.I. was run by bossy women who she felt no longer held her in awe, and the rest of the women were the village hoi polloi. There was no one in the village of her age and station in life, she felt.

She often thought back to her childhood. Their family life had been so happy on the farm. She had collected eggs, helped milk the cows, and been driven around in the back of her Father's open jeep. She had enjoyed making faces at the village children as she had swept by, her hair billowing in the wind. She had helped the cook to bake cakes, and the cleaner to polish and dust. Until she grew older, of course, when she felt these things were beneath her.

The four children had attended a small private school in the town five miles away. They didn't learn too much in the way of Maths, but had Ballet lessons once a week, and Brownies all in school time. Everyone was constantly reminded of the manners befitting young ladies and gentlemen, and social graces were given high priority on the school agenda. French was taught from the age of seven, but nobody ever dreamed of going to France in those days. In winter lacrosse was played enthusiastically on the nearby Recreation ground, and in the summer they played tennis.

At weekends they were allowed, in turns, to have friends to stay. Alison had laughed when one of her friends had observed that the bathroom in the farm was bigger than her own parents lounge. Summer time always seemed to be full of sunshine and running through the fields and woods. They had tents in the garden, and there were always fetes and garden parties to attend. Her parents entertained seldom, they were always so busy on the farm.

Alison loved animals and dreamed of becoming a vet. One Christmas when she was about fourteen she was given a Siamese kitten. She loved him so much that she sneaked him upstairs to bed with her. A few weeks later Alison began to feel very unwell. Normally she was such a robust girl. Her breathing was laboured, and she had developed rashes and itches she had never experienced before. The Doctor looked serious.

"I'm afraid she has developed a severe allergy to animal fur," he told her Mother. "A farm is probably the last place she should be."

The next morning her parents imparted news that was to change her life.

"Your mother and I have decided that you are to go to boarding school for the sake of your health," said her father sternly.

"No way," shrieked Alison. "I am not going to be sent away like some unwanted possession." She turned with an anguished expression towards her mother. Her mother avoided her eyes.

"There is no point in making a fuss," thundered her father. "It's all arranged. You leave next Monday."

From that time onwards Alison felt hatred towards her parents. When they spoke she scowled her reply. Nothing anyone could say would make her feel better. Her sisters and brother laughed at her behind their parent's backs. The very worst thing to happen was that they had taken away her beloved kitten. She screamed, but to no avail, she had been heartlessly given away.

Alison hated boarding school. She felt a great bitterness towards her parents for sending her away. She missed her old school friends. She was rude to her new teachers and uncooperative. She gave up any pretence to try to conform. She was sullen and withdrawn with the other girls, but most of all she was horribly unhappy.

Her first holiday at home soon arrived. Although she was glad to be away from school, Alison enjoyed being as difficult as she could in her home. She refused to become one of the family and spent as much time as she could locked in her room. Her mother tried to plead with her to conform, but Alison, with arms folded tightly across her chest, scowled in reply. She was impossible, nobody could get near her.

Back at school, Alison could no longer be bothered to pay attention to her lessons or her homework. When all the other girls were swatting for their exams, Alison read cheap novels that had been smuggled in to school. For the first time she wondered what it would be like to be in love. She would love to have a boyfriend, she was sure she would find happiness then.

When the long summer holiday arrived, Alison noticed a young, good looking farm labourer who had recently come to work for her father. She brushed her hair, put lip salve on her lips (what a habit this had become), and sauntered casually out into the farmyard.

"Hi," she said sweetly. "Have I seen you here before?"

"No, I've just come to the village. I only know Mary Mason, who lives down the farm cottages, and her family. Her dad's the postman and her ma cooks for your ma."

"I don't think I know Mary, " Alison said softly, amazed at how gorgeous he looked close to.

"She works in the Village pub," explained the young lad. "Anyway, what's your name? I'm Dave."

"Alison," she smiled at him. She could feel her cheeks flushing.

"We'll have to speak again," he said, looking at her with approval. "I'm off to have my lunch. Bye."

Alison could not concentrate on anything. Her mind was full of wondering when she would see Dave again. The next day was cloudy and as Alison crossed the farmyard the heavens opened. She raced for the safety of the hayloft, and almost crashed into Dave as he too ran in for shelter. They stood next to each other panting from the dash for safety and laughing at their bedraggled appearances. How it happened Alison never knew, but she suddenly found he was holding her tightly and kissing her.

After that first romantic encounter, they met secretly as often as possible. Alison knew she was madly in love. Dave told her he loved her too. Life could not have been happier for Alison. She was even able to speak to her parents with a degree of civility.

"Don't you ever tell anyone about us," Dave made her promise. "This is our special secret."

"I know," she replied happily. "I never want us to end."

Over breakfast the one morning her mother announced that the cook needed time off to go and help her daughter choose a wedding dress.

"She's marrying young Dave," explained her mother. Alison felt light headed and ran from the room. She saw Dave coming towards her in his usual jaunty manner. Alison rushed at him, beating her fists on his chest.

"How could you? How could you?" she cried.

"Whoa," he said. "What's got into you?"

Alison explained.

"Oh, don't worry about that. It's you I love, not her. Somehow I've been tricked into marrying her, but it's you I want to be with."

Alison was reassured. She knew her parents would never agree to her marrying Dave so she decided to continue their affair.

Their relationship carried on for weeks, until Dave's honeymoon arrived. When he arrived back to work, Alison found it hard to forget that he had been with Mary. She desperately wanted their relationship to continue, but decided it was getting too dangerous. They had been lucky not to have been discovered, so with a very heavy heart she finished their liaison.

When the cook brought in the photographs of her new grandson to show the family, Alison could not bear to look at them. When Alison saw Dave around the farm she knew she would never recover from her hurt and disappointment. She wondered why life was so unfair. Very occasionally she saw Mary with a pushchair and two older children trailing along beside her. She longed to confront her and tell Mary that it was her, Alison, he really loved. Those children should have belonged to Dave and her, not Mary and Dave.

As the years went by, Alison stayed on the farm to care for her elderly parents. She heard that Dave had run off with his young next door neighbour, leaving Mary with four young children to bring up alone. The day arrived when Alison needed a carer from the village, someone to get her up in the morning and cook breakfast. Someone to get her tea and put her to bed. Mary was sent as her carer, much to Alison's displeasure.

Mary was continually moaning about her hard life, her money worries, and her son in trouble with the police.

"Well, of course," said Alison spitefully, "they never had much of a father to discipline them."

"What do you mean?" demanded Mary. "My Dave was a wonderful, faithful man until that woman put some sort of spell on him. He never looked at another woman throughout our marriage 'til she got her talons in him."

"You'd be surprised!" said Alison maliciously, tapping the side of her nose.

"You don't know anything you sour old spinster," spluttered Mary angrily.

"Ah but I do. Me and Dave were made for each other, and if it hadn't been for you getting pregnant, we had planned to run off together and get married," said Alison triumphantly.

Mary ran from the room screaming, "You wicked old liar."

Alison was found dead a few days later when the man came to read the meter. She had an angelic smile on her face as the Vicar said a prayer over her corpse.

## Christmas Lost

Life was wonderful!  She gazed proudly at the sturdy baby kicking his legs and gnawing his clenched fist as he gurgled happily in his crib.  Her younger children played noisily on the floor with crayons, glue and paper.  Arguments were quickly settled, tears soon wiped away.  The older children squealed as the paper chains they were making to decorate the living room grew longer and longer.  The children had jostled for the position earlier that morning as they had taken turns to stir the Chistmas pudding with an enormous wooden spoon.

A sudden loud hammering at the door interrupted their activities and every head turned towards the intruder.  Her mother in law stood agitated and white faced on the threshold.

'You'd better run down to the pit – I'll mind the children' she panted.

Elizabeth grabbed her coat and shawl, her cheeks suddenly red with dread and her eyes fearful.  Her husband and fifteen year old son had set off for their shift earlier that grey morning.

As she careered down the steep streets, the narrow grey fronted terraced houses on either side appeared like rows of headstones in a cemetery standing to attention, silently letting her past.

At the pit gates the crowds shivered involuntarily with dread in the raw air.  Friends and neighbours lost in their own world of fervent hope, unable to catch each others eye, some sobbing quietly.

'I'm so sorry, a massive explosion below ground.  Nobody could have survived' announced a faltering voice.

# Lord Bingham

"Oh no!" exclaimed Chris. "That call was from Hilda, she wants to stay and bring some friends as well as John and Jennifer. She is writing to explain the situation."

Hilda was Chris's aunt, totally mad and extremely pretentious. Her letter told us that she had met a wonderful man on her recent Mediterranean cruise, and what apparently made him even more wonderful was the fact that he was a real live Lord of the Realm.

Lord Bingham was fascinated by the excavation of the Mary Rose and wished to visit Portsmouth's Historic Dockyard. He had two distant cousins staying with him to whom he would like to introduce a little culture. Aunt Hilda insisted that she wished to be introduced as Chris's cousin, not his aunt as she had told His Lordship a little white lie about her age, and aunt made her sound so old!

By the way, her missive continued, could we please address him as Your Lordship, unless he invites us to do otherwise. We both shook our heads in incredulity. No way, if he was staying as our guest he would be addressed as Nicholas.

The day of the honoured visit arrived. Hilda bustled in, non stop chattering, followed by her long suffering silent husband, John. Trailing behind came pale, sickly daughter Jennifer aged sixteen. Our daughter, Lisa, having not seen Jennifer for a few years, raised her eyebrows in despair at her second cousin's cowed demeanour.

Lord Bingham was introduced with great reverence, and much bowing and scraping by Hilda. He was a tall, tanned brown haired man in his forties. Very upright and polite.

"May I introduce my cousins, Mr. Henry Bingham and Mr. Victor Bingham?" Lord Bingham enquired. Lisa' face lit up at the sight of these two young lively looking lads. Fun might be had after all! They spoke with an attractive Southern Irish burr, and over an evening meal it appeared that following Lord Bingham's recent visit to their home in Ireland, the family seat of the Bingham family, the two boys had come to England for the summer to work before Henry started Law School.

Lord Bingham was a distant relative; they had not met before his summer visit to Ireland. But they had been brought up in a tiny village on the far West coast of Mayo, which was almost cut off from civilisation. Although they lived in the ancient Manor House, the two boys, their two brothers and their mother lived in very straightened circumstances. Whoever of the four brothers was first awake in the morning had the choice of the one wardrobe of clothes, explained Henry.

The first day of their stay was a beautiful sunny summer day. Lord Bingham had arranged a Harbour trip on a private launch. He reeled off the introductions of his guests to the Master of the vessel in a quaint, old fashioned manner giving every one the correct handle of Mr., Mrs., or Miss plus a first name for the unmarried youngsters. A lot of unnecessary bowing was taking place.

Lisa and the two young Irish lads were having a great time joking and laughing. Hilda was in her element fawning all over His Lordship. John and Jennifer sat quietly close together, silently watching the assembled company. Chris was enjoying his role of official photographer of the proceedings

At the end of the boat trip, Lord Bingham announced that tea would be taken in the nearby Hotel. A splendid banquet was waiting, with wine, or tea and coffee. Lord Bingham stood up to make a speech, at which the youngsters visibly winced and suppressed their giggles. The toast was to Henry the Eighth's warship. His Lordship's voice was cultured and authoritative.

"Here's to his rusty old balls," Henry said irreverently much to the amusement of his brother and Lisa. The young trio obviously found the proceedings boring and old fashioned, although they attacked the food and wine with gusto.

Hilda, her eyes brimming with tears at Lord Bingham's benevolence, said His Lordship would like to invite us all to take dinner with him tonight. Wonderful, no cooking! But it took hours for everyone to change and get ready, and lots of wine was consumed while we waited for each other. Lord Bingham appeared in immaculate evening dress, much complimented on by Hilda. The youngsters, in jeans, raised their eyebrows at his appearance. Everyone else was attired in smart casual.

A fleet of taxis arrived to transport us to the posh restaurant. The décor was olde worlde, with stiff white table linen and rows of heavy silver cutlery beside each place setting. A confusing variety of cut glass wine goblets were in front of each person. Silent waiters glided by, attentive to our every need. Ice buckets were laid at intervals down the table, the wine never stopped flowing. Once more His Lordship rose to toast us all individually and thank us for our friendship, hospitality and kindness shown to his nephews.

During the meal, the subject of genealogy and family trees were mentioned. Hilda said her great aunt Mabel had traced their family back to Lord Osborne of Mells in Somerset.

"Never heard that one before," whispered Chris.

"I have it all written down," retorted Hilda with a withering look at Chris.

# Lucy Lightfoot

Gillian drove down the steep, bumpy drive to the ancient flint Manor house. This visit to a remote hamlet in the middle of nowhere would give her the perfect relaxation she needed after the last few hectic weeks. As dusk arrived she walked to the window to draw the curtains. Gillian jumped and shrieked as she looked into the face of a dark haired girl staring back at her through the pane of glass. The fleeting glance she caught of the girl gave her the impression of an expression of great sadness. Gillian tugged the curtains so desperately in her fear that several hooks came off the rail. The girl would have needed a ladder to have been so high up off the ground.

Gillian ran wildly over the uneven floor, down the steep staircase to the Manager's office. She desperately rang the bell for attention.

"Please can I change rooms?" she sobbed.

"What on earth's the matter?" he asked in a concerned manner.

"The face…there was a face at my window" she stammered.

"Oh no," he smiled reassuringly, "that's Lucy Lightfoot. She lived in this farm in the 1820's. We haven't seen her for a long time. Now she's seen who is in her room, she won't bother you again."

"But this is 2009. Is she a ghost?" asked Gillian wiping her eyes. She didn't believe in ghosts, and thought this Lucy person must be someone playing a practical joke. "Tell me about Lucy Lightfoot," she begged the Manager.

"Come and sit in the Dining room, I'll bring you a cup of strong coffee and I'll tell you the tale of Lucy."

"Lucy Lightfoot was the teenage daughter of the farmer who owned this very farmhouse. She was a beautiful girl, but not like other teenagers. She was a loner who didn't mix with people of her own age. She had a black mare that she spent ages grooming and riding. But her greatest love was going into the church and gazing at the effigy of a mediaeval knight. A small dog lay at the feet of the knight. The knight was Edmund Estur whose father was the Lord of the Manor. His father had the effigy commissioned after Edmund didn't return from the Holy Land wars.

Local youths would ask Lucy out but she wasn't interested. When her contemporaries visited neighbouring villages, or attended Harvest dances, Lucy always refused to accompany them. In the end nobody bothered to socialise with her. They just nodded to her in Church on a Sunday.

One gloomy day a local saw Lucy tethering her horse to the rail outside the church. As the rain began to fall heavily she ran quickly for shelter in the porch, and was last seen disappearing into the church. A violent storm raged overhead, and when it abated Lucy's mare was found shivering outside tied to the rail. Lucy was nowhere to be seen. She was never seen again.

Lucy's parents searched desperately for their daughter, so did all the locals, but there was no sign of her anywhere. Some time later Lucy's father sold the farm and moved with his wife to live with their son some distance way. They died heartbroken, not knowing what had happened to their daughter.

Some years later, a historian, who was an authority on the Holy wars, came across an old document which described how Edmund Estur had been so seriously injured in a battle that it was feared he could not survive the journey back to England. Instead he was taken by boat to Cyprus. Defying all the odds, he did survive and settled to life in Cyprus. He met and fell in love with a local girl, named Lucy Lightfoot, and they had a large family and lived comfortably on a farm in Cyprus."

"How strange," murmured Gillian. "Her poor parents. Is the effigy still in the Church?"

"It certainly is, mended too, although you can still see the damage from the storm," replied the Manager.

"If the Church is left open I'll make that my first call tomorrow," said Gillian. "And don't worry about changing my room. I'll be happy to stay put after hearing the tale of Lucy Lightfoot."

# Till Death Us Do …

They met at the Pyramids. It was love at first sight or instant attraction. He worked in the Army Pay Office, alongside her father. She lived with her parents in the Army Quarters in Cairo and worked on the Base as a civilian clerk.

Lloyd was good looking, with black hair, grey eyes and a friendly grin. Elsie was strikingly attractive, with brown eyes, brown hair, and perfect teeth. She was tall and slim, he was only her height, but to her, irresistible. Their first few months together were spent in a whirlwind of passionate encounters after work. Within six months they announced their engagement, much to her mother's disapproval, and four months later they were married.

"Marry in haste, repent at leisure," her mother's voice of doom warned.

Her father had tried to warn her of Lloyd's heavy drinking, but Elsie had only seen him on his best behaviour, well educated, well spoken, reading a French daily newspaper, and taking her to the best open air restaurants. When they were apart it was because he was playing hockey, tennis or billiards with the "boys". Together they were blissfully happy.

Just months after their marriage, Elsie, her mother, and all the other Army wives were sent to the relative safety of South Africa for the duration of the war. Here Elsie soon became bored with her mother's company, and joined some of the younger wives for a night out at the "Blue Slipper" nightclub. A handsome, white uniformed South African Officer asked for a dance, and before long, Elsie was transported back to her single days and loving the attention and flattery of a personable young man.

She did feel a little guilty when she received Lloyd's affectionate letters, but she was quick to blame her predicament upon the Army. After all, she was only young and you couldn't expect a young girl to sit in every night, alone with no social life. The Officer, named

Johnny, called to collect her for a date. He assured her mother that he was merely befriending a lonely wife and he intended no improper behaviour. Her mother's pursed lips and narrowed eyes did nothing to deter Elsie dashing out with Johnny as often as possible.

"It'll all end in tears," she gloomily prophesised, studying the leaves left in Elsie's teacup.

When the letter arrived from Lloyd telling Elsie he was on his way to South Africa, and that they would be sailing home to Britain together. Elsie viewed it with mixed emotions. It had been fun being free in sunny South Africa. War torn Britain and grey skies would not be so welcome.

Not long after they arrived home, Elsie found she was pregnant. Lloyd was sure he would be having a son and was already calling him David to his parents in his letters. He wanted to introduce her to his family as soon as possible. His was a huge family, out of nine brothers and sisters six were still alive.

"You'll love my mother," he confidently announced.

In the gloom of a rainy day they arrived at his parent's home. Lloyd's brothers, sisters and their families were crowded by the door for a first glimpse of the wife that everyone had yet to meet. Elsie felt the disapproving glances from his dowdy looking sisters as they stared at her very high heels and smart fashionable clothes, and makeup. She could almost hear them whispering "and her pregnant too."

His mother came towards her with a false smile, cold grey eyes glinting and said

"How nice to see you at last Rita." In the confusion and babble, Elsie smiled politely ignoring this slip of memory. Her father in law was very welcoming, but Elsie was surprised to hear her well spoken husband lapsing into a strong local dialect when chatting with his family. It didn't suit him, she thought.

His brother in law, Harold, was full of plans for their stay- all revolving around nights at the Rugby Club, pub crawls, and Old Boys Reunions. He had missed Lloyd's company for years, and didn't want to waste a second of the evenings they had before them.

"Your husband's the life and soul of every night out," he gleefully confided in the less than enthusiastic Elsie. She knew these night's out would be men only and did not relish the idea of spending miserable, long evenings with his mother, gazing into the fire and drinking endless cups of tea.

One night she did accompany Lloyd, her brother and sister in law and Lloyd to a dance. She was amazed when Lloyd ran over to the band, grabbed a violin from one of the musicians and played along with the band with gusto.

"I didn't know he played the violin," she whispered to her sister in law.

"Oh, yes, we all had to learn an instrument," Carrie replied. "Mother was all for education. I played the piano and got to Grade 8."

"Who is Rita? Your mother keeps calling me Rita, and Lloyd says it's because she is old and confused." Elsie whispered again.

"Some friend of the family from long ago, take no notice," replied Carrie, who was not overly fond of her mother.

The men came home drunk and disorderly most nights, and Elsie was glad to escape to Chester. They settled in a flat, part of a house and Lloyd often came home very drunk. Sometimes Elsie had to drag him along the passage from the front door, even though she was very pregnant. The landlady tutted at the sight. At other times he was incoherent, and as soon as his dinner was put in front of him, he would fall forward at the table, head into plate of food. In the mornings he was mortified, sometimes crying, and promising not to come home like that again.

After the birth of their first daughter, they moved again and things were better between them. Although disappointed that the first baby had been a girl, Lloyd proved to be an excellent father. Soon a second baby followed, another girl. Lloyd cried with disappointment, but was hopeful of being third time lucky.

Elsie was thrilled to be returning to the Isle of Wight to live, while Lloyd travelled weekly to Winchester. He was able to have his nights of drinking with the boys during weekdays, and be home at weekends to help with the children. One day he announced that he was being posted to Accra, and hoped Elsie would join him there. No chance, she said. She felt happy where she was and saw a little freedom on the horizon.

When she received the telegram starkly telling her how full of regret the Army felt to have to inform her of Lloyd's death due too malaria, Elsie knew her life was about to change forever. It was not long after this that she was sent the small brown paper parcel that held Lloyd's diary, written when he was in his last year at school. It was full of books he had read, films he had seen, sports he had played, friends calling round. And on nearly every page appeared Rita. Sometimes they were in love, sometimes quarrels were mentioned, they broke up then got back together with monotonous regularity. At the end of the diary Lloyd wrote of his intention of getting engaged that summer.

Years later Rita appeared in Elsie's in laws back garden on a visit from New Zealand where she had fled on hearing of Lloyd's marriage. Elsie was scathing in her asides to her daughters.

"She' certainly no oil painting, no wonder he didn't marry her!"

# Works by Barbara McMeekin

# Déjà Vu

I opened the door and walked through the opened curtains into the consulting room. My stomach tightened as usual. Immediately I saw the familiar bed with its blue strip of paper ready for the next patient. I saw the basin, chair and other medical supplies. I knew the routine well.

The nurse followed me in and said, "Strip to the waist. Mr. Knowles will be in soon." She then left through the other door at the side of the room. I put my bag down on the chair and took off my jumper and bra automatically. I sat down on the edge of the bed wishing that we had had more time to park the car so that Alan was alongside me in time for my name to be called.

It wasn't too long before the side door opened and Mr. Knowles appeared wearing a smug, detached expression. He wished me a good afternoon with a half-hearted handshake, and then said "Would you lie down please so that I can examine you."

Obediently I did as he requested and lay there as he explored my left breast with its unsightly double scar. He then quickly checked the right breast in a dismissive way before saying "your scarring is as expected and we could consider reconstruction."

I lay there thinking, wondering, waiting and so had said nothing until this point. "But, but…" I stammered. "I thought I had come here for the results of the biopsy I had two weeks ago on my right breast."

This seemed to puzzle Mr. Knowles for a moment. He then reached for my notes and began fingering through. "I beg your pardon? When did you have the biopsy?" he asked for confirmation.

I told him the date as he began a more thorough search for the information.

"I had my annual mammogram in July and was recalled. I didn't have the further ultra sound scan and biopsy until I came back from my holiday. Today I thought I was getting the result." I remembered thinking that I was going to have my holiday come what may and that I would stay positive and enjoy it as much as possible, even though what I might have to face hung over me like a huge dark cloud.

I slid off the bed and stood next to him as he found the latest information. When Mr. Knowles said he had found the results he began to tell me the details in medical jargon before sitting himself down realising that he should have been more prepared. Results like mine are usually given with back-up from his medical team. Last time I had Mr. Knowles, his deputy, a specialist breast care nurse and the duty nurse in the room before I was told. As he sat there he said "I'm so sorry. I'm so sorry."

At first I wasn't sure what he had read out but as I observed his body language and heard those words "I'm so sorry" I realised my hopes and positive thoughts had been dashed. I stood back and leaned against the bed, shock and disbelief creeping through my head. Then it dawned on me. It was back. I had breast cancer again.

"Is there anyone with you today?" he asked.

"Yes, my husband. He couldn't find anywhere to park so he said he would join me in the waiting room."

Mr. Knowles stood up and went back through the side door. I was left alone. I couldn't believe it. I didn't want to believe it. I wanted to shout "it's not fair" and "why me?" I was not only stunned but shocked. I put my bra and jumper back on even more automatically.

It wasn't long before the main door opened and in walked Alan and the same nurse. This time she stayed in the room and Alan came over to me. I was rocking to and fro. I think from the stress. He could see immediately that the news wasn't good. He put his arms round me and held me as I cradled into him. I couldn't speak. I felt devastated. I felt almost the same as I did the last time but somehow it seemed worse.

The side door opened and in walked Mr. Knowles. This time his face held a grim expression. As he shook Alan's hand he began, "Mr. Brown. I'm really sorry but fate has repeated itself, and this time it is much more serious. Your wife had a rare cancer last time but I'm afraid that the cancer this time is a much more virulent strain. It's hormone responsive and as such is aggressive in its nature."

I sat there half listening and thinking that it just couldn't be. Five years ago I had been told that it would take a long time before it recurred. Five years was not a long time. I thought I would be in remission at least fifteen or twenty years before it could or would strike again.

Alan, like last time, began asking questions. "Will Mary need further treatment after her surgery?" I was in too much shock to ask anything.

"I'm afraid so, yes. We will do a full lymph node clearance and if the cancer hasn't spread then I'll be advising chemotherapy and more radiotherapy. If the cancer has seeped through the lymph nodes then we'll have to reassess the situation following the results."

I was still half listening but the realisation was sinking in.

"How soon will the operation be?" asked Alan.

"We'll arrange the operation as soon as possible. If you would like to take Mary home we will send you the details, but it should be by the end of this week." Mr. Knowles replied as he looked at the nurse and handed her my file. He then bade us goodbye and shook Alan's hand again. He touched my shoulder and left.

I picked up my bag and followed Alan out of the door. I walked almost like a zombie. I couldn't speak. I felt numb. All sorts of thoughts were feeding in and out of my brain but they made no sense. I didn't speak in the car all the way home. I nodded or shook my head to answer Alan. Once home I collapsed on the couch. Alan made a drink of very hot, sweet tea. I drank it without tasting it. But then slowly I began to function again.

It was the phone ringing which brought me out of my dazed state. Hearing the sound meant that I had to tell my family, my friends and my boss the outcome. I had to say the words and face another battle for life. Only after the first call did I allow myself the luxury of tears. After that Alan answered the phone and left me to come to terms with what the future held.

It was another five years on last week. I saw Mr. Knowles for the first time since that day. The consultation went well. He examined me, discussed my progress and assured me that everything was fine.

As I drove home I began thinking. I have undergone surgery again and endured both chemotherapy and radiotherapy. I regained my stamina and returned to full time work until I retired eighteen months ago. I have survived and I am a survivor. There can be life after cancer. I am one of the lucky ones. Life is good. I now have three more grandchildren and I am enjoying life. Everyday problems are not worth worrying about. Instead I stay positive and count my blessings daily.

# Hypocrisy or Betrayal

The radio was on and as the voice of Diana Ross filled the room, she remembered back to the day when she found out. She stopped knitting.

Her parents were the epitome of a perfect couple. But their silver wedding anniversary had been their downfall. They'd only married three months before she was born. She was a love-child. Her mother didn't wear white but clothing coupons were still used then. She knew the date of the marriage but no-one mentioned which year. The anniversary was always remembered so she never questioned.

As she listened she felt the betrayal once again. I was brainwashed into staying pure until I married. I had to, otherwise I would be spoiled goods and he would know. But I committed the moral sin; I went ahead with the marriage. I was trapped.

The song ended and she tried to resume her knitting. Knit one purl one was in danger of becoming weave one deceive one. Everyone makes mistakes. But a wrong stitch can be undone and no-one would be wiser. A dropped stitch can be picked up and no-one would know. My parents were hypocrites, she thought. She had been deceived. She now realised that she could have broken the engagement and probably avoided divorce. As it turned out she wasn't pregnant. Would it have been so wrong to have had more than one lover?

# Limericks

As Christmas Eve drew near,
Santa began to feel queer.
But he loaded his sleigh
with a song and a sway,
before downing another large beer.

Christmas is a time for fun,
once festivities have begun.
Santa hats, party frocks,
knitted jumpers, silly socks.
Though hangovers are bound to come.

# Love Bites

Jim answered his radio, belted up and started the engine. Jasper was already in his crate and Jim knew from the glimpse in his rear view inside mirror that he was braced for the journey. He knew Jasper was always alert and would know instinctively that they were about to undertake the next job. Jim and Jasper were known as the JJ team and they had been on duty for seven hours of the ten hour shift. By six o'clock natural daylight was dimming as the evening drew in, just enough light if there were lucky.

Jim set off at speed staying in radio control, manoeuvring and meandering expertly along the roads avoiding all the traffic through the town. He was heading for the crossroads on the A234, just before the fork towards Waterside Down where on one of the corners was an eighteenth century thatched cottage, the place of the reported incident.

Jim screeched to a standstill, glad he had arrived without using the siren. Moving with the agility of a hunter ready to attack, he ran round to the back door of the van, sprang open the crate and clipped the lead onto Jasper's collar. Together they reached the front door in a manner of seconds. It was slightly ajar and all seemed quiet. Jim pulled back on the lead giving Jasper a visual command to be still and silent, before he slowly and carefully pushed back the door. It was too late. The burglar having heard the squeal of the brakes had scarpered out through the back door.

Jim and Jasper hurried through the hall towards the back just in time to see the culprit clambering over the far hedge. Jasper began barking as they ran in pursuit down the garden. He had already picked up the scent but he was too short to scale over the hedge without help. "Wait!" Jim ordered.

Although excited Jasper sat down as Jim unleashed him and lifted him carefully up and over the top of the uneven, rough privet. Because of the height and unevenness Jasper wobbled as he landed, but being focussed on the job shook himself and began his chase. Jim followed. As he had to swing himself over the hedge he landed in a heap jarring his ankle. Closing his mind to the excruciating pain in his foot he picked himself up and began running across the rough open field to catch up. All the time he kept his eyes peeled on the target and at the same time watched Jasper gaining ground.

Sensing he was in danger of being caught the burglar looked behind him. He saw them both and realised that Jasper was getting too close for comfort. In an attempt to escape he aimed then hurled his bag at the dog. Jim read his body language and afraid of putting Jasper in danger called out, "Down boy!" Some of the sound was carried by the wind and despite Jasper obeying immediately the bag caught his ribcage momentarily winding him.

The burglar lost some of his balance in his effort at stopping the dog and began to stumble helplessly on the uneven terrain. However he quickly recovered and began running again. Realising that the man was not carrying a dangerous weapon, Jim shouted, "Stop!" Give yourself up or the dog will strike."

The man ignored his warning, so Jim yelled, "Attack."

Jasper sprang into action and raced towards him. As he caught up with him he leapt upwards, sunk his teeth through his clothes to bite his arm. Losing his balance the man fell to the ground. Jasper held on and shook his head each time the man tried to hit his face screaming all the time "Aagh, Gerroff me. Aagh, Gerroff me."

Within moments Jim reached them both.

"Ger 'im off me," he screamed, "before he rips my' bleeding arm off."

Taking his handcuffs out of his pocket Jim gave Jasper the command, "Leave."

He obeyed immediately. The man clutched his bitten arm and writhed about in agony. Jim knelt down on one knee with his other in position ready to restrain him if necessary. He read him his rights and arrested him before cuffing him. Jim then helped him to stand ignoring his protests.

As they walked back towards the house Jim radioed control inquiring where his back-up was. Within seconds he heard and saw another blue light approaching. Two policemen met the party and Jim handed the man over. They escorted him to their car and Jim took Jasper back to his van. Jasper sat by the door looking up at Jim with complete unquestionable faithfulness and devotion. He knew he had done well and was waiting for his reward. Jim bent down and stroked his loving loyal pal before reaching into the van to pick up the much chewed rubber ball. "Here Jasper. You've earned this. We're a great team you and me."

Jasper took it and began playing. Each time he dropped it Jim would throw it for him to retrieve. After a while Jim said, "Time to go buddy. Our shift isn't over yet." As Jasper settled in his crate Jim was thinking how lucky it was that only a bag and not a weapon had been used. Once again the JJ team had come up trumps and once again the thought of losing his soul mate crossed his mind but only for a moment before dismissing the image.

# The Hotel

"I've done it. After all this time I've finally done it. I've booked a long weekend in Blackpool, though the hotel is now called 'The Central Seaview'." I said reaching for the print-out of the confirmation details.

"At long last," Richard replied. "It's only taken the best part of forty five years. So I suppose you want a medal or at least a pat on the back?"

"Ha, ha, very funny. I don't think. You know it was very sad and tragic. It wouldn't have happened now. Not with our health and safety rules and PC'ness."

"I know, you've not been ready to go back before now. Come here," Richard said as he putting his arm round me "Let's open a bottle, and I'll run you a bath so that you can go and relax."

As he ran my bath I took my glass of Rioja, undressed ready to slip into the water. When I entered the bathroom I saw lit candles on every corner and recognised my favourite bubble bath as the mountain of soap suds bubbled higher than the rim. The scene invited me in and as I lay there my mind went back to that last fateful time I was at the same hotel.

After a while I heard Richard call from the bottom of the stairs. "Would you like a fill-up?

"That would be lovely. I'm getting out now so I'll be down in a sec." I didn't take long to join him in the lounge. He refilled my glass and I sat on the couch with my tucked up legs up. I felt relaxed and comfortable in my pyjamas and slippers.

Richard had noticed. "The bath worked then?"

"Yes," thinking that the wine probably helped as well.

"Do you think you'll recognise the hotel? Blackpool must have changed radically since the middle of the sixties."

"I suppose so, but it should be fairly easy. I'm sure once we get to the turn off at Manchester Road it'll only need us to look for the name. Those grand steps up to the front door won't have been altered much and there's the passageway on one side leading to the road at the back."

"Did you say it had changed its name?"

"I did. It's not 'The Seaview Hotel' anymore, but I don't know when it became 'The Central Seaview'. It was probably after it was sold when it was refurbished and needed a fresh identity to avoid any stigma."

"Just remind me how old you were when you first worked there."

"Sixteen. I enjoyed it mostly. Being a receptionist and waiting on were fine except but I didn't always enjoy being a char maid. It wasn't the best of jobs, but during the four summer seasons I was there Mrs. Jackson was either let down or found it hard to get staff so I had to muck in."

"I guess hotel life was very different then."

"Yes, though by 1964 things began to change and many hotels modernised with them. Most began giving options when booking reservations. Bed and breakfast or bed/breakfast and evening meal became very popular, and were offered as well as the traditional full board. Mrs. Jackson though was stuck in a time warp, and as time went by Mrs. Jackson refused to change anything or alter the hotel in any way. She insisted on keeping everything the same as it had always been."

"Some people find it difficult to adapt. It knocks their security. They like feeling safe and are afraid to take risks."

"I agree, but I think her trouble was also linked with her background. Don't forget she was born in 1900, and as the daughter of a mill owner from Clitheroe she had had a very privileged Victorian upbringing. Even up to the time of her downfall she was a very regal and proud woman. When she married Mr. Jackson, he had been the family's chauffer and when they later bought the hotel Mrs. Jackson became the proprietor and Mr. Jackson became a gofer. He was very rarely included in any decision making. I'm sure that was something she must have regretted right up to her death twelve months later."

"You maybe spot on there, but you'll never know cos it sounds as though she wouldn't have ever admitted it."

We sat there for a few minutes each lost in our own world and enjoying the wine. "Do you know which job I liked best? It was the banging of the gong at every meal time. I'd take the gong and begin hitting the copper drum, building up the sound and rhythm to a crescendo followed by six loud bangs. Before each meal Agnes, the main waitress, and I changed into our black long-sleeved dress, with a white starched lace-edged apron over the top. It had one of those bibs pinned neatly across the chest. We wore a white stiff hat on our heads and had to fix it with hair clips. I felt the part in that uniform. I think I've still got a photo of us somewhere."

"I've seen it and very fetching you looked my dear."

"There's no need to be cheeky."

He grinned as I carried on. "It was our job to allocate the patrons to their table and they would sit there for the duration of their stay. No-one was able to choose where they could sit. Mind you they couldn't choose what to eat either. The breakfast menu began with porridge or cereal, followed by a cooked fry-up plus toast. The men always had two eggs and the ladies were given one. Dinner was always served at 12.00 prompt. There were always three courses, usually hot, followed by either tea or coffee. High tea was then served at 4.30 prompt and was usually made up of sandwiches followed by cakes, a selection arranged on a three-tiered cake stand."

I took another sip of wine and still holding the glass I said, "I used to hate breakfasts if anyone hadn't come down. I remember very clearly that it was served between 7.30 and 9.00 am. It was always me who was sent to knock on the door and remind them. I hated it, especially if I had to go up a second time then tell Mrs. Jackson that they didn't want any. I used to get really flustered in front of her and then feel embarrassed when they came down and she spoke to them. I used to hope she wouldn't see them, but she must have had antennae pointed at her door."

"She must have realised they had appetites only for each other,"Richard said with a grin on his face. "How many rooms were there?"

"There were twenty four mixed-sized rooms on three floors. Each one was furnished but they weren't luxurious by any means. Each one had a white basin but the toilets and bathrooms were shared on each floor. I remember seeing queues especially before breakfast. All the beds had white cotton sheets, woollen blankets and eiderdowns. She didn't decorate either and slowly each room was becoming more old-fashioned and dilapidated. You'd think that changing the linen and bedding would have helped the laundry. But she wouldn't listen to any suggestions on how to improve standards."

"But surely she could see for herself, couldn't she?"

"No. Mrs. Jackson suffered badly with gout so she couldn't see the deterioration for herself, and as she would not replace her existing stock, consider the introduction of showers or modernising the bathroom areas the hotel became very much worse for wear and shabby. I can still see the letters W C on each panel of the old doors. They were so stark and uninviting."

"She did supervise the dining room though, but again she was reluctant to alter anything. The cutlery, tea pots, coffee pots, milk jugs, sugar basins, serviette rings, jam pots and marmalade pots were all silver. One of my jobs was to polish them when they tarnished. The plates, cups and saucers were all white bone china and the table cloths and serviettes were all white starched cotton. So the dining room also began to look very outdated as well, especially when you compared it to the other hotels along the promenade."

"Maybe, but it was the chef who was to blame for the inevitable downfall?"

"Oh yes. Jim. Yes he was the one who abused the ordering and the cooking. But Mrs. Jackson allowed him more and more of his own way mostly because she was unable to go downstairs to the kitchen and she trusted him. Over the four years I worked there I saw how the kitchen deteriorated. Mr. Jackson knew though. I remember that the year before he had refused to eat anything that came from downstairs to the point were he was taken into hospital with pernicious anaemia. But even that didn't make Mrs. Jackson realise that there was a problem with Jim."

"Or she didn't want to see it," Richard interrupted. "I thought she was the one who served up the food."

"She did. Food was sent up on the dumb waiter and she plated it up. She served the food as best as she could but it didn't always look appetising, and she saw the leftovers and dirty dishes before they were sent down the dumb waiter. But again she would be unwilling to listen to any suggestions of change or improvement."

"I'm glad I never stayed then, though I would've liked to have been a fly on the wall when the heavy mob arrived," said Richard trying to keep the conversation light-hearted.

"I wish I'd have been able to be a fly and not part of it," I replied. "It was the third week in August '67 when food was particularly unappetising not only to look at but to taste. One or two people began to have tummy upsets and then more were becoming ill. To this day I'm not sure who called the Health Department. I remember one couple that week that were not only shocked but appalled to learn that Jim was the chef after seeing him going to Mrs. Jackson's room. He would come upstairs and walk past the main stairwell and dining room usually still wearing his filthy apron and smoking a cigarette. He had become so overweight and slovenly that I would cringe if I was asked who he was. I used to get so embarrassed."

"If he was so bad surely she wouldn't have told him to have at least taken his apron off and try to look more respectable," said Richard.

"She probably did but he knew she couldn't go down to see him so he would have simply ignored her. He was a horrible man and just as stubborn as she was." I put my glass down and changed positions. "I'll always remember the day it happened. It was about 3pm on the Thursday when two men accompanied by a policeman walked through the entrance door. They pushed it open and I asked to see Mrs. Jackson. I knocked on her door and showed them in. One of them produced papers allowing them access to search the hotel kitchen. I stood by the open door listening. I was then asked to show them where the kitchen was. My stomach knotted as I took them downstairs. I went back to see the Jackson's, who sat there looking shocked and alarmed, even Mr. Jackson.

I knew exactly what they would find downstairs. The men found filth not only covering all the surfaces, but the floor was dirty with raw food and cooked debris. The main fridge was the worst. All the food was badly contaminated. The delivery of yesterday's fresh salmon was already going green with mould, milk and cream was sour, leftover food was uncovered and the smell was putrid. You just can't imagine what it was like."

"I've got a good imagination. I've been to some dirty places in my time especially when I worked for the Council," Richard reflected. "What happened then?"

"Well, the men came back upstairs and spoke to the Jackson's. They told them what they had found and that they were closing the hotel with immediate effect. Anyone staying there would be found alternative accommodation. They also told them that they would be prosecuted."

"What happened to you and the rest of the staff?"

"After they'd left we were all summoned to Mrs. Jackson's room. Although she was very shocked and upset she told us with as much composure and dignity as she could gather that the hotel was closing and we would be paid til the end of the week. We were then dismissed and I know I had an awful sense of numbness walking slowly back to my room. I did cry but not until later on, after I'd phoned my Dad. I went home the next day. It was ages before I found another job."

"Did you go to the court with them?"

"No. I couldn't face it. We weren't needed as witnesses. There was enough evidence collected by the health inspectors," I said. "I believe that Mrs. Jackson looked solemn though but still tried to keep an air of self-respect. It was in the papers and was even on the TV but not hyped up like news nowadays."

"Were they sentenced?" Richard asked.

"No. They were given a very heavy fine since their age and health were taken into account. They ended up with no money though even after the hotel was fumigated and eventually sold. They ended up renting a small one bedroom flat where they lived quietly until Mrs. Jackson died about twelve months later. It was so sad. She lost all her friends as well. I think only one person ever visited her. I went to see her before I moved down South. She seemed to have shrunk and I always carried a feeling of guilt. Maybe I could have done more but I don't think I could have done any more than I did. She wouldn't listen and at the end of the day the buck stopped with her."

"Well, it's all in the past and you've moved on. Now any more lingering gremlins we will be swallowed up with new sights, sea and what's the other thing beginning with 's'?"

"I can't think. It can't be Sangria cos we're not going to Spain," I replied throwing a cushion at him.

# Works by Helen Lartham

# Acoustic Landscape

A dark sky cast long shadows on the Derbyshire hills turning everything into strange and unfamiliar territory. Charlie was by now almost completely deaf, as his days came and went in a haze of work and chaos he was now gradually becoming aware that he was losing his acoustic landscape. He hadn't needed his eyes to know when he was approaching the brook just outside the village, because song thrushes had nested for generations in the old horse chestnut tree. He had learnt to distinguish their song from all other birds in the same way he knew the chatter of each of his fourteen children. Now everything was gradually fading into silence.

He had walked with undivided determination the three miles from Caddesden to Breadsal loaded with everything his family could need for the coming winter. Mary, the quickest and his favourite, was the first to greet him. Never was the welcome home warmer than on his return from market. Once inside his flock of children descended on to the heavily leaden bags, their excitement crashing around his head like a jumble of pure confusion.

'Did you get me the shoes dad? Please let me look.' Mary spoke slowly forming her words with exaggerated movements of rounded lips.

After a hesitation of only a moment, Charlie carefully placed an old pair of boys' boots on the table with infinite pride.

'But Dad these are boys' boots I can't wear these, everyone will laugh at me.'

Mary's round face crumbled into a look of bitter disappointment with a strange intensity that only she could muster. Charlie didn't need to speak the words; his look of bewildered anger was enough to send her to a quiet corner of the crowded room. Although she was still an innocent girl, Mary knew that her mother would not have brought her boys boots to wear. Memories of her mother were now becoming hazy. All except the picture she kept by her bed to gaze at with the aid of a secret candle in the dark of night. This picture showed a plump good natured woman who liked to cook. When she was confined upstairs producing her many children she would keep cakes under her bed to give to the children when they popped in, concerned. Mary had heard the stories of how her mother would welcome all the tramps and undesirables of the village; she would call them in for refreshment and a chat, offer them help, then send them on their way. After all, she saw them as Gypsies, like her own family had been. The death of her eldest son in the Great War was her undoing and she died a month after he was declared missing in action.

With the first stirrings of life the whole house awoke to a new day. In no time at all the place was buzzing like a well run army camp. Everyone had their job to do. Mary's was to peel an enormous pan of spuds that would sit quietly simmering all morning on the black leaded stove. At first she objected to this.

'But Wilfred only has to polish Dad's shoes, that don't take any time at all.' Mary had pleaded.

'He's a boy.' Torrie the eldest would always reply.

This came with a rap across the knuckles. Family life gave Mary her first grounding in injustice. Life was going to be hard; she had best learn that now.

A sharp knock on the door sent John the youngest bounding happily from the room, they so rarely had visitors. He came back at the same rushing pace flushed with pride at his important news. Then he paused for a moment before turning his face to his father knowing, as young as he was that Charlie would need to see his face to understand. Now he guessed his father might not like his news after all.

'Mrs Fletcher to see you Dad.' John panted.

Charlie unravelled his long limbs slowly and levered himself upright with the look of a fighter weary with a battle he can never hope to win. He took the portly, but sharp nosed Mrs Fletcher, into the best room brushing layers of dust from the furniture as he passed. Fourteen pairs of ears jostled for position as soon as the door was closed.

'I'll get straight to the point. Mrs Hopkins says she can give your Margaret a good home,' Mrs Fletcher said then hesitated looking for a moment directly into Charlie's eyes as if to judge his mood. When she was met with stony silence, Mrs Fletcher continued undaunted.

'You know her John has got diphtheria, you will do them both a favour. Margaret can help with the baby and in her turn Ma Hopkins will do her best by Margaret. You have to think of her best interests, she can give Margaret a much better start in life than you. Why don't you admit you can't manage with all these children?'

Charlie rose in a deliberate act of dismissal.

'Well, I'm sorry enough for Ma Hopkins, Margaret will, of course be happy to help out, when she's finished her work here mind. But you'll understand I give Margaret everything she needs here in her own home. She's my concern not Mrs Hopkins.'

Mrs Fletcher rose with an exasperated sigh and smoothed her apron with brisk agitated movements.

'If that's your final word then I'll be off, but don't expect this to be an ending. You will be seeing me again. I only want what's best for these children.'

She manoeuvred her large frame, with as much dignity as she could muster, around the maze of old furniture crowding the best room and headed quietly for the door. Charlie felt a momentary pang of regret; she meant well if only she would stop trying to interfere, he would quite like the woman.

'John will see you out, goodbye and good fortune to you Mrs Fletcher.' His voice was now soft and courteous.

A deflated gaggle of children clustered around the door muttering disappointedly amongst them.

'What does Mrs Hopkins want our Margaret for anyway, she's lazy, an' on cold nights she takes all the blankets for herself,' John said while doing a couple of cartwheels around the room, with no better reason than to relieve his pent up energy, before adding,

'Margaret doesn't even want to play or anything she's too busy reading her books.'

The children all decided that adults were very strange creatures indeed. Everyone had expected some interesting news and now felt badly let down.

John pleaded. 'Let's go out and find Hannah. We can play in the big horse chestnut.'

Charlie slipped, out barely noticed by the family to start his days work. Today he would be repairing a dry stone wall belonging to the farm at Morley. He could never bring himself to tell the others but he knew he didn't really belong inside the house. Out here in the free air, he belonged. It was his world. Everything worked without noise. No chaos of rushing bodies, no half heard words or steaming pans of stew to scald himself on. Picking up speed with easy strides he was soon past the grey stone village hall and the crusty old apple tree, now as bare as winter earth.

With his work done it was already late afternoon and a thick clinging fog was wrapping itself around everything even Charlie's mind. Putting everything away in his bag he noticed a gooey stream of blood trickling down his right hand. A prickly cold panic sent his whole body rigid. His hands were the only things that separated him and his family from starvation, he must not damage them. All he had in life came through work. Looking at his long white fingers he knew the skill that lived in them could be turned to any use. He had been in turn a carpenter, a shoe smith and a saddler. Each apprenticeship cut short by his father who always seemed to find out when Charlie's pay day came and made sure he had his wages to buy more drink. So Charlie had always moved on until the day came when there were no more fathers to steal his pay. Then he met his Mary. After that life seemed to unfold into its own pattern and he was content. Then came the dark pit of grief it had taken him years to crawl out of after his Mary's death. He was satisfied to go along with what ever came next as long as he had his children.

Charlie decided he must get back home as soon as possible, the dense fog was chilling him to the bone and he had to bandage his hand. He would take the short cut across the railway track at the Moor, which was the quickest way home. His mind was beginning to work faster now but the fog was so thick he couldn't see his own hand in front of his eyes. He climbed down the steep bank gingerly and now he guessed he had reached the railway crossing as he could just make out the gleam of metal through the mist. The rail beneath his feet seemed to be vibrating slightly. Surely there was no train crossing here on a Thursday afternoon. Walking slowly on he felt as if there was a strange power holding him back causing his feet to drag on the ground. The cold had turned his feet so numb they were hardly under his control. His mind was playing tricks on him. He thought he could hear the high pitched whistle of a train engine. This was impossible. His heart began to beat faster and faster in rhythm with the track beneath his feet. He must get off this track, he must move quicker. But his feet wouldn't obey his commands and he stumbled to the ground just in time to see a large black train loom out of the mist and before his startled brain could register pain the blackness became complete.

The whole long day, Charlie's children were far too busy working and playing to think of their father. At last, with the sky turning a starry black, Mary began to shift uneasily at the tea table.

'Dad should be back by now.' She turned to Torrie fixing her with eyes made large with anxiety, 'Can we go and look for him, please?'

They searched all the land between Breadsal and Morton knowing he was supposed to be mending the wall at the top farm. The blackness of night now was beginning to close around the children, strange noises sent them scurrying backwards and forwards. Even the ground seemed to be echoing to the cries of frantic voices levelled at the full pitch of young lungs. To anyone watching from a distance the family began to resemble a pack of hunting wolves howling with rage in their attempt to find their missing leader.

It was Margaret who was the first to come upon a group of people standing by the railway track at the moor. They were gathered silently around what looked like a sack on the track. To the stricken eyes of the children they appeared like statues, wooden and lifeless suspended in time. It was Mrs Hopkins who brought them back to the cold reality of world.

'It's the Taylor kids don't let them get any closer they mustn't see their father like this,' she said.

Not one of the fourteen children could say how they came to be back into their own home that night. They were to learn later that Mrs Hopkins led them all the way home making each hold the hand of the other like a ghostly crocodile snaking it's way slowly back to it's den to heal it's wounds. Now the storm was over they just sat or laid for hours cold and still, as if death had taken them all too.

Torrie the eldest was the first to emerge from the void of grief and she soon took command.

'Margaret and Henry you can clear away the tea things, Sally you can put out the fire in the boiler,' she ordered.

They all rushed to obey her in grateful relief. Someone was taking control. Soon the whole house was put to rights and the little ones were washed for bed. With everyone stowed away for the night an uneasy peace descended on the home. For many weeks to come Mrs Hopkins came and cooked for them and Mrs Fletcher came to clean. The more she insisted they must go to other homes the more determined they became to stay together. After all Torrie, at fifteen, was a capable mother. All the children knew, even the young ones, it would not have been their father's wish to have them scattered to the winds, like leaves in a storm.

# Cat

I pick up the phone slowly, heart beating fast. This is something I don't do every day, shopping my neighbour to the authorities. I glance at my emaciated cat, his once rotund frame now resembling a bucket of bones, up turned on the cushion, and I resolve to make the call.

'Hello, I would like to report my neighbour, Mr Jenkins for the neglect of my cat. He agreed to look after him while I was away; Achilles is now completely emaciated, close to death. Will you send someone round? I want him locked up.'

I return to feeding Achilles with a syringe, a few drops of milk at a time into the corner of his mouth. I keep going all night, by the morning he can raise his head, and I know all will be well.

Today, I leave the county court. It was I, not my neighbour who suffered prosecution. They claimed it was my responsibility. I should never have left my cat with Mr Jenkins. He couldn't stay in my house to supervise his eating because of the cat fur allergy he never told me about. Apparently, I am lucky to get the £500 fine and not a prison sentence. As soon as I enter my home I am greeted by a chorus of insistent meows as all ten of my rescue cats demand to be fed. I was always destined to care for these abused creatures but never realised till Mr Jenkins neglected Achilles.

# Depend on me

Jo walked briskly, purposefully down the opposite road to the one which she had intended. It was catching sight of John's face that caused her sudden change of direction. It was those once familiar features that had been haunting her for the past year. Only they had the power to send her scurrying. She had to risk another look, yes it was John. There he was walking down the same street on the same day, at the same time as her, could this be just coincidence?

A tingling shot of excitement throbbed through her body sending adrenaline coursing through her veins, and at the same time causing intense irritation. Why was she behaving like a school girl? Just the sight of him transported her back to her teenage infatuation; she resented this power he had over her. She was too old for this. What was he doing here anyway? The dark granite stone walls of the British museum loomed before her like a comforting old friend.

She was about to make her way home when she spied John entering the building. This, she decided, was a blessing. She could follow him to find out what he was up to in the anonymity of those long museum corridors bedecked with artefacts, and with plenty of places to hide. At the same time she could take the opportunity to explore this museum that she had never before had the chance to explore. Once inside Jo soon lost sight of him and decided to look around the floor with the ancient Egyptian exhibits. She soon become tired of trying to elbow and battle her way to the front of queues to glimpse one more sarcophagus, without the time or peace to read the information and understand what she was looking at before she was expected to move on. As she turned from the mummified remains of a long dead Pharaoh, she spotted him. There he was, his long body leaning gracefully against a display cabinet, almost as if he had placed himself there like another exhibit for her to gaze upon and scrutinise from all angles, for her own exclusive pleasure. For a couple of seconds she wished she could attract his attention, she just wanted to spend some time alone with him. The next moment all she wanted to do was escape, run away as fast as she could with her heart pounding, fit to burst. After all he was her nephew Ryan's best friend and many years younger than her, just how many she had no idea, and she wasn't about to ask. After all she hadn't seen him all year, in fact not since she had told him how worried she'd been; worried she would never walk again after her accident. He had seemed oddly ill at ease in her company then, and had just slipped away not answering her letters.

Jo froze as John walked across the hall in her direction. Oh god he had spotted her.

'Jo, how great to see you,' John said.

'You'd written?' He looked surprised when she asked him why he hadn't written back. 'I'm afraid I moved address and no one sent your letters on to me,' he added but she was unsure if she believed him.

He flashed Jo a coy half smile. Jo found herself mumbling, 'Sorry, I have to go, have to meet an old friend, I'll be late.'

She was just reaching the door when she found him blocking the way, looking at her intently.

'What's the matter?' John asked.

His large grey eyes full of concern. Jo felt her determination dissolve; this only made her angry with herself. This wasn't a good idea was it? What would Ryan feel about her following his best friend around and meeting him alone, but then did she really care? Besides she was, more than likely; just about to make a fool of herself.

She found herself saying, 'John, I'm sorry but I have to go, otherwise I really will be late.'

But John held firm, his face, normally handsome, now suffused with a brilliant crimson. He anxiously ran stubby fingers through his thick brown hair.

'We need to talk.' Now there was a note of panic in his voice 'Look, lets go to the coffee shop I need to ask you a favour.'

'I told you I have to go, I haven't got the time,' Jo interjected briskly and started to walk around him to the exit. However he wasn't budging, he was still blocking her way out.

Sighing in exasperation he said, 'For goodness sake, what is so urgent that you can't give me five minutes of your time?'

She hesitated for a second and then her resolve evaporated completely. 'OK, I can give you five minutes.'

A quarter of an hour later found them sitting in a cosy corner of the canteen with slabs of fruit cake and steaming cups of tea. At last Jo was able to hold the cup with a steady hand and ask, 'What is so urgent that you need to talk to me now when you haven't answered my letters all year?'

John had the grace to look sheepish as he replied, 'I told you I didn't reply to your letters because I never received them, and to be honest, I was feeling guilty. I disappeared after your accident because I felt responsible for what happened to you.'

Jo spluttered over her tea, this was news to her.

'Go on' she encouraged.

'Well, you fell on the stairs because you were the worse for drink and you only got drunk because I encouraged you,' he said.

Jo felt relief and excitement. At last she was going to find out what had been going on with him. And she thought she knew the answer, he had obviously been feeling the same about her as she felt about him otherwise why would he get her drunk? The answer came swiftly, but it was an explanation that she did not like.

'John, why did you get me drunk?' She injected as much anger into her voice as possible.

John concentrated on looking at a dirty smudge mark on the table and avoided her eyes.

'Well, I needed to ask you something and I thought if you were relaxed and happy, it might help. I needed to ask if you would lend me some money. I mean, we're good friends aren't we, so I thought you might be willing to help.'

Jo's heart plunged into her stomach, so it was all about money was it?

'What did you need the money for?' she asked, her voice cracking like ice.

'I needed your help because I'm afraid I had got myself into a bit of a mess over my finances, lost some money gambling, and the debts just seemed to pile up.'

Jo gazed coolly into his eyes and thought for the first time that he looked weak and desperate, and then Jo saw it. As the cuff of his sleeve pulled up when he stretched out his arm, the red track marks of inflamed veins tinged with a long blue bruise down the length of his arm standing out against his pale skin. Those were needle marks. Betting on the horses my foot, he's a junkie that's what he needed the money for, drugs. That's what he still needs now. Perhaps, he knows he can always depend on me. For the first time she smiled warmly at him, now he was going to need her help more than anyone else. Jo lightly tapped his hand.

'Why don't you come back to my place then we can talk about the possibility of my loaning you some money, in comfort.'

John rose with a slight smile and followed Jo slowly across the canteen and out into the cold streets.

# Dereliction of Duty

When I saw her lying there somehow shrivelled, in that hospital bed, I knew Mum needed help. There was only ever me so I sat quietly by her bed. I watched her drift into consciousness.

'Oh Caroline,' Mum said looking over my shoulder, 'where's Janice, she promised to come.'

I answered swiftly,

'Mum. You know how busy she is at work right now.'

As in a consolation I proffered her my present of fruit I knew she liked,

'Here these are for you.'

Mother waved her arm dismissively towards her locker,

'Someone else might want them. I never liked apricots.'

Then she pointed to her get well card, with two simpering kittens playing with a ball of wool gazing smugly at me from the picture,

'Isn't it lovely, Janice sent it today?' But she added in a worried voice, 'I was the first down and the last to come back from surgery. I've asked if something went wrong, but they won't tell me anything.'

As I left Sister approached me,

'Excuse me we need a quiet word. I'm afraid during the operation on your mother's wisdom teeth we discovered cancer of the mouth. The doctor believes we have caught it early and we are sure your mother will make a full recovery, but we are waiting for a loved one to be present before we tell her. Can you come back tomorrow when doctor makes his rounds?'

I nodded dumbly. On reaching home I rang my sister. Someone must tell her I decided. Her boyfriend answered, speaking angrily,

'She had to go to that dreadful party on her own. How come you're never here when Janice needs you?'

# Son of Mine

Peter Marshall lifted the stump of his right arm and gave it a rub to ease the ache. His hair had thinned lately to a wispy grey. His face was now lined with many wrinkles, resembling a parched landscape, grainy as a desert. Looking up his eyes sparkled like bitter blue icicles as he motioned for the man who had just entered the room to sit opposite. Andrew Johnston's face in many ways mirrored Peters own, it was lean and lined, except his eyes might once have held a twinkle. They weren't bright now; they hadn't sparkled since the vicious attack that had rendered his son fighting for his life in hospital.

Peter spat out the words as quickly as possible, so they might not sully his lips.

'So you have found me at last. I take it you haven't notified the police, otherwise you would not be here now. It's such a pity I didn't call the police myself, straight after the 'accident', but I was too traumatized. I suppose I mistakenly thought then that I owed you some loyalty! Owed you something for those years of so called, friendship. I let the police think that the winch was mine. It was the biggest mistake of my life. '

Andrew Fisher stood up to his full height banged his fist on the table and shouted. 'You bastard, my son is in hospital because of you.'

Peter held up his arm to interrupt Andrew tirade.

'You have no one to blame but yourself.'

Andrew continued as if Peter hadn't spoken.

'Why did you have to do that to his arm, to make him like yourself? He nearly bled to death. I take it this was your punishment. Why the hell didn't you take my arm?'

Peter circled the table staring intently at Andrew,

'I wanted to remove your right arm like you removed mine. But your son Mitch, he's your right hand man isn't he? Very close aren't you? But you won't go to the police, will you, because if you do, you know I'll prosecute you for negligence. I'll take you for every penny you have. After all, it was your fault that winch failed, that my arm was crushed, and my life was ruined.'

Peters tone became almost contemplative,

'Once I'd recovered from the accident I went from the hospital to the rehabilitation centre, so I could start a new life as a disabled person, learn how to cope. Only it's a fiction, isn't it? I will never be normal again.'

Andrew added angrily, 'I expect I'll find this out for myself, Mitch will be in a place like that soon enough, thanks to you.'

Peter continued undaunted,

'Yes it felt good in the in the centre, but out here in the real world the only jobs employers want you for, if you're like me, is stuffing envelopes and pushing leaflets through letterboxes. I lost my well paid job, spiralled into depression, began drinking, and then came the final blow, my wife left me. So you see I have nothing left to lose, and my one reason for living is to make you understand, to make you experience what I went through. To see you broken is the only way for me to find any peace.'

Andrew backed towards the door and turned to shout,

'You crazy bastard. It was an accident, you God Damn Son-of-Bitch. Watch my lips, it was an accident! I didn't know the stupid winch was broken. I hadn't used it for years, but you would insist you needed my winch. You were so God Damn obsessed with that car. That precious Lotus became everything to you. How long have we been friends? One stupid mistake and friendship means nothing to you?'

Peter spoke, calmer now but went on with a definite gloat in his voice,

'One stupid mistake, you say, but a mistake that cost me everything. Well, perhaps now you have paid, or should I say Mitch has paid on your behalf? All the greater punishment for you, I feel. But you're wrong you know. I 'm not crazy. I planned all this carefully, from finding the right drug to sedate Mitch so I could remove his arm without killing him, to paying that tramp to loiter outside your house for a few days before my attack. I wanted you see him, remember and later tell the police. Of course it was pure luck that he had connections with the criminal community, and so led the police down the wrong path. All that surveillance to strike when I knew Mitch would be alone. Hardly the work of a deranged madman!'

Andrew now reached the door, silently he tried the door handle, the door wasn't locked he smiled satisfied. Then he turned to shout and curse Peter,

'What the hell do you want with me? Why did you agree to meet with me?'

Peter laughed softly and said, 'All in good time, first, I want to know how you discovered it was me who attacked Mitch?'

Andrew relaxed as he sat down on the chair.

'Let's just say, I had tip off. We have a mutual friend who got suspicious. I was pointed in the right direction. Then I remembered the rumours I'd heard about you being hurt. I kept quiet about your accident I didn't want any repercussions after all, but once I guessed it was you it was only a matter of time before I found out the truth.'

'Now all I need to know is why did you come here? What did you hope to gain?' Peter asked.

Andrew fixed Peter with an intense stare,

'I needed to know why? It was important for me to know why you would do this to my son. After all it was all my fault'

Peter smiled.

'Wasn't it obvious? Like I said, I had to take your right hand. It was justice. Everything was out of balance'. Peter smoothed down his tie and pushed the hair out of his eyes with shaking fingers.

'It disturbed me. I had to make things right, make you know what it is like to lose control of your life'.

Andrew shouted angrily,

'Well, it wasn't obvious to me, why you mutilated my son, instead of coming after me? But then I'm not a sick fuck like you am I? I've heard all I needed to hear. I've got it all recorded here on this handy little machine and the police will be very interested to have this confession from your own lips.'

Peter sniggered,

'So how much good do you think that will do you? If I go down so will you. I think you had better give that thing to me don't you? I'll make sure it doesn't get into the wrong hands.'

Andrew put the recording device back into his pocket and faced Peter.

'We'll both go down you say, well, not quite. Today at ten o clock, my son died of his injuries. You may have used an untraceable mobile to phone for an ambulance so he would be rescued before he bled to death, but you weren't clever enough to use a sterile scalpel. He developed septicaemia. So you see, like you, I have nothing left to lose. So I'll be keeping this and I hope you rot in jail.'

Andrew smiled grimly as he added,

'By the way, you might like to know that Mitch was your son. Yes, Janice told me about your affair before she left and she confessed that Mitch was not my blood son but yours. I need you to understand this, Mitch was mine, in all the ways that count, and I made sure he never knew about you. He called for me at hospital in the end...he called me Dad.' Andrew's voice trailed off.

The venom sounded in Peter voice.

'You knew I always wanted a son. And you never told me! You knew how jealous I was that you had the one thing in life I wanted a son.'

Andrew let his bitterness and grief spill into his voice,

'Of course, now it gives me the greatest pleasure to know that you and Joy were never blessed.'

A flash of metal glinted in the half lit room, and Andrew fell crumpled to the ground as a bullet from Peter's revolver hit his left shoulder. The wail of police sirens sent the neighbours scurrying to their windows.

Twenty four hours later and Andrew come round from the life saving operation that had repaired his shattered bone and sinew. He found his ex wife Janice sitting by his bed. He looked at her with some apprehension, her face pale and anxious. Within a few hours he was conscious enough to be burning with questions.

'Have they got him?'

Janice leaned over and brushed his hand fleetingly with hers, the touch was feather light.

'Yes. He's locked up in a police cell as we speak.'

Andrew leaned over and spoke with a husky voice,

'I'll always be grateful to you for coming up with the plan and for supporting me. But you waited a long time, you were playing a dangerous game, he nearly killed me.'

Janice sighed. 'Don't forget Mitch was my son too. The police were getting nowhere and we needed a confession. I knew he wouldn't be able to resist gloating. I knew you could make him tell us about Mitch. Anyway he always was a rotten shot.'

Later that evening when Janice returned to Andrew's bedside she reached into her bag and brought out a photo album full of pictures of their son. Snaps taken when he was two minutes old still glistening with amniotic fluid, and when they turned the last page he was beaming proud in his graduation robes. When Andrew had finally sated himself with memories of his son, he slept, his face worn but blessedly peaceful. Janice put the book away and slipped into the dark night.

# Works by Bryan Hodgekins

# The Bridge

A few years ago during my summer holiday I thought I would go for a few days walking. The forecast was promising. That was important, as I was taking my pup tent.

I dug out some maps and while browsing through them I noticed I had picked up an old one, which contained a list of all the disused railways.

Looking at them closely I found one that was not to far from where I lived. It ran from the town of Fareham and along up to Alton, near Winchester. It was what they called the Meon Valley line. I thought it would be a good idea to have a go at walking the length of it. So the next day I packed up my kit and went on my way.

I got the train to Fareham. When I got there I asked the stationmaster if I could start my walk from Fareham. He was a jolly chap and only too pleased to help. But he had to tell me I couldn't as the rail or path as it was then, and still is, was a little way farther up the main line. He was very sorry for not being much help, but went on to tell me that the best way was to catch a bus to Wickham and start from there.

I thanked him and did as he said.

When I arrived at Wickham I asked a man where would be the best place for me to get onto the old railway track. He didn't only tell me, he took me there. While we headed in the direction of the Meon valley line He told me about the line and its history. And the very famous people that travelled on it. For example Winston Churchill and General Eisenhower, travelling to Southwick house to plan the D Day Landing. He then went on to tell me about a ghost. I listened to him for a moment. Then had a little laugh and told him:

"I don't go along with that stuff."

We eventually got to a small gate, which opened on to a path that led up to the track. He then said,

"Will you be camping there? If so you might find some odd things by an old bridge. Don't let it worry you though."

I thanked him for his help, and carried on my way. I went through the gate and climbed a very steep slippery path. I finally got to the top of the bank after a lot of slipping and sliding, and there before me were the remains of the railway.

It was how one would expect to find it all overgrown with very large shrubs and trees that had been let to run wild along the track. I say track, as it was more of a narrow path. I walked for a while until the path started to get a little wider. I wondered why that was, so I looked around for a short while, until I came across what looked like the remains of a platform. Although I did not think that it was a main one, as it looked more like a stopping point for the farmers to load up. There was very little of it only little bit of concrete buried in the undergrowth.

After a little more rummaging I continued on my way along the path for about 5 miles, when I came to an arched bridge made of stone and bricks. It looked very much like it was a cattle crossing as it went from one field to another. I noticed the area around the bridge was quite flat and dry, and as it getting late I decided to set down my tent for the night

I was still on the south side of the bridge where I hoped the sun would show itself in the morning.

After having a cup of tea and something to eat, I had a stroll along the embankments to see what was around, when I saw a rickety old farmhouse just to the side of the bridge. It didn't look occupied, so, as I am by nature, inquisitive, I climbed down the bank to have a closer look.

I had a wander around it hoping to find something of interest, when to my surprise I heard a shout coming from the building "What you doing?" he said.

I looked to see who it was, when I saw a scruffy old man leaning out of a window. I say window. It was more like just a hole in the wall, with the window hanging out on one hinge.

"I'm very sorry." I said. "I thought the house was empty."

"Well it ain't is it?" He said in a disagreeable voice.

I pondered for a moment wondering what to say to him. When I went to move off, he then called after me saying.

"Anyway what is it you want?" And by the sound of his voice his attitude had changed. He was very nearly nice.

"Well I can do with some water." I said.

I then heard a woman's voice from inside the house.

"Behave your self you silly old fart." She said.

Then she came to the door. She was an old lady with very long grey hair. She looked as if she had a deformity of the spine as she was so bent; she had to use a walking stick to keep her from falling over.

"Don't you go taking any notice of him young man; he can be a bit cantankerous at times. Showing off he is anyway" she went on to say. "If you be wanting some water there's a well round back, you be helping yourself to what you want."

I thanked her very much and went to go back to my tent when she called after me.

"You camping then?"

"Yes." I replied. "I'm up by that old bridge on the old track."

"Are you?" she questioned with alarm in her voice. "You don't want to be camping there. It'll be full moon to night, and it is the time."

I wondered what she was talking about. What has a full moon and the time got to do with it?

I thanked her and said,

"I will remember what you said."

She then called after me.

"Don't you be saying I didn't warn you? And if you have a problem, you come down here, we'll look after you."

While walking back I did think about what she has said, also it came to my mind what the chap had said down at Wickham. It didn't worry me, well not a lot, only I did feel a little mystified.

While drinking my tea I began to realise that it was so much darker here than down by the house, and I couldn't help noticing the moon rising up over the trees, and yes it was a full moon. Thinking about what I'd been told I decided to have a look around by the bridge to try and see what it was she was talking about. When I came across something that turned my stomach over, there were lots of mutilated rabbits and birds hanging on nearby trees. They looked like they had been mutilated before they died for there was so much blood, that it could only have happened while they were still alive.

What a horrible thing to do, I thought. Then to add to the scene I felt a cold shiver run down my back, as I wondered if it had something to do with witchcraft. Then I thought of the old lady. Would I need her, like she said? But was she one of them? One of what? I went on to think? And who were them? Was she a witch?

I felt all of a sudden very lonely. Like the poor soul in the Wicker Man film. Would they use me? What for? My mind had now taken over and was running my brain into the world of the psychic. I wanted to pack up my kit and move to somewhere else. But what I had not noticed, it was very much darker for everything now had gone black. I looked along the track to see if it was safe to move on without falling into hidden hole, or tumbling down the steep banks into a deep muddy bog that was along side the track. I could see the trees from each side of the track getting closer to each other, blocking out most of the moonlight, so putting any thoughts of moving out of my head.

I went back to my tent put my battery powered light on and made another cup of tea, thinking all the time about what I had just seen and wondering if what the old lady said was true. I will admit the very thought of it put fear into me and to make me wonder what I was going to see next. I switched the radio on, hoping it would give me some sort of company. I zipped up the flap on the tent, and then got in to my sleeping bag. I tried to sleep, but I found the thoughts in my head kept me wondering what strange thing was about to enter my tent. Then the light started to fade, which created ghostly shadows on the side of the tent. Then my light completely failed, I wanted to light the stove, but I knew that if I had the flap closed it would be dangerous. I had then a choice to ether turn the stove off or open the flap.

I groped around in my kit bag hoping to find my torch. I realised that I could not keep it on all night. I chose to save it but kept it close to me.

After a while without noticing it I nodded off to sleep. Only to be woken up by some strange sounds. I listened very carefully to what it was, as it was a sound like wind, but not quite. For the reflections of the trees on my tent were not moving. The sound then started to get louder. Then louder again until it became deafening until my ears wanted to burst. I then recognised it.

It was chanting.

I wanted to get out of my tent to see what was going on but my fear now had got greater than my thoughts of going out side. Then suddenly the chanting stopped, leaving an agonizing silence. I sat just listening, then shortly afterwards I heard, in the far of distance a sound I recognised. It was the whistle of an old steam train. Where was it coming from? I slowly and quietly unzipped the tent and then even more slowly looked out through the flap. I looked each way. There was nothing. Everything was quiet and still.

I tried to put my fear to one side hoping I could raise enough courage to get out of the tent. Then I heard the whistle again this time it sounded closer. I slowly crawled out, all the time looking each way in case some monster crept up on me, as one would do if you're scared out of your wits.

I lit my torch and proceeded towards the bridge with caution. Why I chose that way I don't know, for the thought of the poor animals came to my head, and the chanting. My mind then started putting them together, bringing back the fear. I then heard the train whistle again, this time it sounded a little louder. I tried to think where it was coming from. For all I knew it was coming from a distance, from the other side of the bridge.

I wanted to venture on. I stopped. For the scene had changed. It was no longer a grass and bramble covered path, and the trees were cut back.

Then I had another shock. On the ground were railway tracks.

I covered my face with my hands, thinking I was hallucinating, but no, for when I took my hands away, it was still there. I then shone my torch on and directed it to the lines. There was no reflection, as if they weren't really there. I then walked on to the other side of the bridge. I stood on the line, only to find my foot had gone straight though it. I then began to think that I was having a nightmare, and all that I was looking at was not really there.

I wanted to wake up. I covered my face again. I turned around to go back to the south side of the bridge and wondered what I was going to see next. I dropped my hands from my face. Only to see tall figures in a line, all dressed in black robes. Then from there black hoods came that chanting again getting heavier and deeper. I wanted to run away, but found I was frozen to the spot I looked to the bridge and I saw movement there. Standing over to one side of the bridge was a figure. I noticed it was shorter than the others and there was a long black dress beneath a cloak. It was a woman. Her face was covered by a black hood, which was attached to the cloak that hung down to her feet. I wondered if she was like the rest of the scene. Not really there.

She walked slowly by me until I could see her face. She was looking at me. There was no expression. I tried to smile. Then I realised I was not there in her world. I realised she could not see me. By now the chanting had gone to a high pitch making me again cover my ears. The train whistle pierced the chanting. It was getting closer and closer. I saw its lights coming very fast around a tight bend in the track. I turned my head only to see the woman slowly walk up on to the bridge and stand in the middle. The train was heading straight for me with flame and sparks bursting out of it chimney like a dragon of old. But I was transfixed, still glued to the spot all the time not believing what I was seeing. I then pulled my senses together and dived off the track and looked up as the train screamed past me and watched helplessly as the lady threw herself off the bridge into the path of the train. There was a scream that blended in with the chanting of the sound of screeching brakes and the whistle of the train making me almost go blind with fear.

Then I heard nothing, silence. The train had gone I saw the track disappear back of up the old railway line. I looked to see if the chanters where still there, only to see then walking in single file into the darkness. Leaving everything back to the way it was.

I wondered if I would come out of this nightmare. That's if I was in one, I was still in the same spot looking into nothing. I shook myself, still wondering if it really happened. I managed to free myself from my mind, and then ran back to my tent, zipped up the flap and got into my sleeping bag, all the time thinking about what I had seen.

I woke the next morning. The sun was shining while I made a cup of tea. I tried to put the nightmare out of my mind. Thinking it could not have been real, until I went to put my boots on. They were covered in mud and slime. Then I found my trousers were covered in grass marks and mud, there was also rip down one side. What the hell went on? I thought.

I got dressed and walked to where it all happened. The animals had all gone. I could see the patch of grass where I landed while jumping out of the way of the train. I then decided to pack up and leave. I went down along the road this time.

Later I from the safety of the library I found that a woman had committed suicide on that bridge by throwing herself in front of a train back in the late 19<sup>th</sup> century.

# The Cat

I am what is called a jobbing electrician, and spend most of my time doing jobs that aren't too big. I work mainly for estate agents. This involves going around houses that have recently come on the market that need the electric either putting right, or testing. I need to make sure the existing installation is in keeping with the current regulations.

One of the first jobs I was asked to do had come from a solicitor. When I enquired at the estate agents about this job, they told me that they only obtained jobs from solicitors when they concerned an estate that had been involved in a will. The estate agent continued that on this occasion the solicitor had not been very helpful. He knew nothing about the work to be done, or about the property. The only information he could give was the address. He added that it was a very old house, built sometime in the middle of the eighteenth century.

"I'm sorry I can't give you more information, Mike," he said. "I think the best thing you can do is go round to the house and take a look at it. The address is 13, Willow Road. Give me a ring before you go, and I can get Bob to meet you there. He's the guy who looks after any building work, at the moment. If you don't mind, would it be possible for you to go round there this afternoon, say about two o'clock? You'll find the keys in the front office. See you later."

After hearing his words, I got a very strong feeling that something was being hidden from me. I thought that whatever it was, I'd soon find out.

The house was situated in what you would call an up market area. It was very nice, except that all the houses had names rather that numbers. This is a bit of a bind when you are trying to find a particular house. I finally found it after a lot of bother including having to get in and out of the car, asking passers by where number thirteen was, to no avail. When I asked a little old man where number thirteen was, he gave me a strange look, almost as if I were an alien or something. He didn't say anything at first, only pointed to a place that was completely covered by over grown hedges and very large trees. Seeing his expression, I couldn't help but ask. "Is there a problem?"

He stood and looked in the direction of the house for a moment, while tapping his walking stick loudly on the pavement. But he didn't answer me directly.

"Are you going to be working there?" he eventually asked me.

"Yes" I replied. "Why?"

He then said in almost a whisper.

"The last men who went in there to do some work only stayed for twenty minutes or so. The last time I saw them they were backing out of the drive, as fast as you like. They didn't even stop to close the gate."

He then tipped his hat, and with a cheeky smile said goodbye. He continued on his way. I watched him for a while as he pottered off down the road.

I turned aside from him and directed my attention to the jungle that surrounded the house. All the time I was thinking about what the old boy had said. I seriously wondered what had I let myself in for? But my thoughts were soon interrupted by someone beeping their horn. I shouted at the driver. "Keep your hair on."

I climbed into my van and drove into the driveway. After turning off the engine I sat trying to get a bearing on the house, but all I could see were trees. I got out of the van and walked on slowly in the direction of where I thought the house might be. I tried to follow what I could see of the path, but it was heavily over grown with long lengths of ivy and roots coming from the forest of trees. I heard the sound of gravel underneath my shoe, and I guessed I might at least be on what was left of the path, which may, or may not be heading towards the house. Following a turn in the path, I saw the house. With a start, I remembered the keys had been left in the van. I went back for them but I didn't get into the van completely, I just sat in the seat with one foot still on the ground. I looked down as I thought I had seen a movement on the ground. It seemed to be coming towards me. I couldn't see what it was but it looked like the undergrowth was moving. My first thought was that it must have been a mouse crawling in it. To my surprise, I felt something crawling up my leg, but I couldn't see what it was, so I panicked. I leant back in my seat and tried to prevent my wild imagination from taking over. Then whatever it was landed on my lap. I wanted to scream. I could feel it, but couldn't see it. I felt perspiration breaking out all over my head and body. There was a sound, which sounded like a purring. As if from nowhere, a large black cat appeared.

"Where did you come from?" I shouted.

The shout must have frightened him, for he quickly disappeared. I felt him leap off my lap and heard him land on to the ground, but nothing else. I thought for a moment that I might be going mad. I got out of the van and had a look around. I felt spits of rain, which were coming from a very dark cloud that was looming overhead. I could see the trees taking on the colour of the clouds, making the surrounding garden change into a black the colour. Following this there was a large sheet of lightning and a heavy roll of thunder. The clouds opened up. I ran back to my van, only to find it surrounded by water, causing a foul smell from the ground. I sat in the van and wondered what to do next, when I heard a car horn beeping followed by a flash of lights. I immediately knew it must be Bob. Thank god! I thought, as by then my mind was in turmoil.

I could see Bob in my rear view mirror. He was a short man with big arms and shoulders. He looked fat, but I could see it was all muscle just like the pictures of the medieval archers that I had seen. He got out of his car and ran frantically towards my van. He quickly jumped in to get out of the rain.

"God's truth, its raining cat and dogs," he said.

When I heard the word cats, it immediately struck a chord in my mind. Holding out his hand he said,

"Hello Mike I'm Bob."

"Wotcha Bob." I replied, "Glad to see you."

Little did he know just how glad I was to see him! I chose not to say anything about the vanishing cat, thinking that he would agree with my feeling that I had gone round the bend.

"Have you had a chance to look around yet? Mind you, I don't think we're going to see much in this weather," Bob added.

"I've only just found the house, and what with all these trees and undergrowth I haven't seen much. With out looking too hard, I'm beginning to think we've got a big job on here. That's without us seeing the house properly yet." I said.

"Hang on Mike, I think it's stopped raining," said Bob.

"Right then, let's see what we've let ourselves in for," I said, as we got out of the car. I looked up at the sky and noticed the heavy clouds were still there making the garden very dark and threatening.

"The garden's in a bit of a state. Although it looks as if at one time it might have been, what you might say, grand. Still I haven't come here to look at the garden. Where's those house keys Mike?"

"In this bag, Bob," I said as I opened the bag, wondering what was in it, as it was quite heavy.

"Cor! Stone me! They look like they come from Wormwood scrubs!" Bob said with a laugh. "Can't see too much of the house with all these trees blocking the view. I think we'd better bring the torches. Better watch it Mike, there's loads of green slime all over the deck," Bob added. Then we heard a noise.

"Blimey, what was that?" I said, feeling nervous.

"Oh! A flaming cat," he replied, which reminded me of my earlier encounter with the cat. I tried to clear my mind of anything spooky.

"I hate cats," I shouted. "Always getting your feet, and jumping under the floorboards, when you're trying to work."

Bob laughed and said. "Right, here we are Mike. Looks as if it's straight out of one of those old times horror movies don't it? You know, what's his name?" He paused for a moment.

"Alfred Hitchcock," I said knowingly.

"That's him," replied Bob. "I hate it if I've got something on the tip of my tongue and I can't think of it. Don't you Mike?"

I didn't answer him. I looked at the very large house, as Bob said; it looked as if it had come straight out of some horror movie. As I looked up at the front of the house, I could see a very tall tower with a pointed roof and narrow windows at the side. They appeared to be the thin slits they built in castle walls for shooting arrows out. There were two windows that made the house look like it had eyes. The rest of the house looked as spooky as this tower. Bob decided to have a look around the outside of the building.

This left me having to go into the house by myself. I admit I wasn't too happy about it and quickly made sure my torch was working. I lowered my gaze from the house to the ground and was startled by the same cat that had come into my van earlier. It was sitting looking up at me. Now why would he be sitting there? I thought there's no one living here? I decided I better make sure he didn't get in the house otherwise I'd be all day looking for the menace.

"Hello mate. You all right then?" I asked, feeling foolish talking to a dumb animal. I gave it a stroke.

"I hate cats," I told him. "Well, I don't really. It's just that you lot keep pinching my fish out of the pond and getting under the floorboards when I'm trying to do some wiring. Now listen cat, there's no good you snuggling up too me, I've got to get in to this house and I don't want you coming in with me." I gave the animal a push, and looked at the bunch of keys. I decided it was a big door so it must be opened with the biggest key. I was right. The lock was a bit stiff, so I went to fetch something to free it up.

"Now you stay there cat. I want you where I can see you. I don't want you to be buggering about like you did in my van," I told him. I turned and looked at the path that led back to the van. It looked spookier without Bob. I didn't want to go back down there alone. With all those trees surrounding me where things could be hiding! But I had to do it, so I took a deep breath and ran as fast as I could. I ran back just as fast with the WD40. Cur! Those hinges needed a lot of oil. I realised I'd forgotten about the cat.

I looked around and wondered where he was? Sod it, I thought; I'll be all day finding him in this huge great house. I entered into the big hall.

"Would you look at those stairs!" I said to myself. "Can't see the point of having two sets of stairs going to the same place though?"

It was a bit dark, and it felt like there were eyes looking at me.

"Bob you still there?" I shouted.

"Yes. Why?" He called.

"Well don't go too far away, 'cause I'm getting the creeps in here."

"You daft sod," he replied with a loud laugh.

Now don't let your imagination run away with you, I thought. I wished I had brought my mate in with me. I tried to switch the lights on. There must be a switch somewhere I reasoned, but then I looked at the fittings. Those light fitting aren't electric, they're gas. Oh no, I cussed to myself. That mean they've got no electric mains. I decided to have a look around to make sure. If there were any they'd be in the basement, I reasoned with a sigh. I found what looked like the door. It was a bit stiff so I put my shoulder to it. That's when the stink hit me. It nearly made me pass out. It smelt like a rotten corpse. I hoped there wasn't one down there.

A loud rustling made me jump.

"Who's there?" I shouted in a frightened voice. "Is that you Bob?"

There was no answer. The cat crept in meowing, and made straight for my leg. It was purring and snuggling up against me. That flaming cat again put the wind up me.

"You little squirt," I said. "Anyway how'd you get down here? You must have jumped through a broken window." I flicked my torch around expecting to see broken glass.

"Hello, where's he gone? All the doors are closed. He must have gone up stairs." I mused and decided to look around.

"Bob you still there?" I shouted.

No answer.

"Where's my torch? Right then. These stairs are a bit difficult. Better be careful Mike. Remember you're on your own… Why did I think that?

Now I've put the wind up myself again…what with the gloom, and that horrible stink." I murmured.

Well I couldn't find any electrics, only gas. I wanted to get out of there before that smell killed me. As I started to climb out of the cellar, I noticed there were no broken windows. So I stopped to think how that cat got in? There must be another hole somewhere else, I thought. The cellar was empty so I had a look at the rest of the house. Wow, this was posh, nicely furnished, it must have cost a few bob, I thought. I wondered if the rest of the rooms were the same. It must have been a posh lot who had lived in here.

I thought, oh yes, I'd better ring the Gov, to let him know we're here. But there was something wrong with the mobile. It was ringing but he wasn't answering. I tried to leave a message on his answer machine but that wasn't working either. I tried again. I decided it might be a bad reception so I went outside and try once more. When it didn't work I thought I would try ringing from the road. Suddenly, I thought hello, what's happened to the garden? It was all scruffy when we got here. Now it's all nice and smart. There must have been a gardener in, but no, we haven't been here that long.

"Bob! You there," I shouted loudly, but there was still no answer. I thought I'd have a look round for him.

"Bob!" I kept calling, but got no response.

I'm not going mad, am I? I thought.

Then I saw that cat again. I'll make sure he stays outside this time... I heard a different noise. I could hear children playing. What they doing in here? I wondered. They were playing with the cat and they were all dressed in funny clothes, in an old fashioned way.

"Hello. Should you kids be in here?" I asked. They're didn't answer. Then I said. "Is it all right for you to be playing in here?"

They were looking at me, I could see their lips moving, but couldn't hear them! Then suddenly they were gone. Where did they go? I wondered. That cat was still there though. I decided something weird was going on here, so I decided to lock up and go tell the governor.

"Bob I'm going back to the office. You coming?" I shouted. I wondered where he was.

"Where'd I put the keys?" I said out loud and realised with despair that I'd left them on the window ledge.

"Oh no not you again. Please don't get yourself locked in. And don't go down to the basement" I said, and I watched as he went and did go down. That was all I needed after having the wind put up me. Chasing a blooming cat around. But I supposed I had better go and get him.

"Come on mate, I know you're down there. Now stop messing me about.

Where are you? ... Where did you go? Come on where're you hiding? I saw you come down here. Hello what's that old box? I didn't see it there before.

I thought this room was empty." I spoke more to try to calm myself than get the cat out of hiding. The box wasn't locked. I decided to take it up to the daylight and take those nails out the latches. The lid was a bit rusty.

"God's truth. It's where that bloody smell is coming from. What is it?" I said as I prised the lid off. I jumped back seeing the tufts of fur.

"It's a cat! Poor thing. Some rotten bugger must have locked it in. Poor sod.

I'd better bury you in the garden. I've got a shovel in the van. Come on puss, let's give you a descent burial," I whispered.

I went out into the garden carrying the box and thought he would like to be buried under an old tree. I was glad the gardener had come round and made the garden neat and tidy, a lot nicer for the cat to be buried in a well tended garden.

"There we are my old mate. Sorry about us humans, but we're not all the same. I suppose you're off to your cat heaven. You'll be happy there," I said, shoving the earth on top of the box.

I went back into the house, had a last look around and decided to lock u, calling Bob as I went. Coming back outside and slamming the door just to make sure it was closed, I turned around. Hello, what happening? The garden's gone back to being all scruffy again.

"Bob" I called in a panic. "You there?"

"Yes I'm here. What's the problem?" He said.

"I think some ones taking the piss or something."

"Why?" Bob asked.

"Did you see those kids?" I asked

"No. What kids?"

"They were playing in the garden." I said. This time I began to think Bob might be having a bit of joke at my expense. So to make sure he didn't think I was going off my head, I changed the subject.

"Have you seen that cat?"

# Little Ragged Sisters

They call our Mum a whore, I don't know what for.
Now she's gone off with that Mister
never mind, I'll look after you little sister.
They give her money for what she calls love,
she don't buy much grub though
she spends it in the pub.
She said she does love us,
it's because she ain't got no money
and she says we're always hungry...

I'm cold
Look at them stars ain't they a show,
they say they're more shiny when we've had snow.
I've heard Angels live up in the sky.
I bet they ain't hungry, I bet they don't cry.

If I were an Angel little sister
I could do lots of things for you.
Just think, I could fly down from the sky,
and bring you lots of food.
I could fly to that big shop at the top of the street.
I'd ask God for some money and buy you some sweets.
I'd make you look pretty with silver and gold,
Then take you to heaven.

Just imagine it
Don't cry little sister
don't go to sleep
I know you're cold.

## Sticky Bun

This is a true story of not to long past,

about a poor family and Christmas coming up fast.

That year had been a struggle with lots of bills to pay,

the family watched their savings slowing melt away.

The parent told the children that Christmas won't be much fun,

for all they had in the larder was a sausage and a sticky bun.

They said that Santa won't be coming this year.

And the house might be a bit sad.

The children took it kindly and said. 'We love you mum and dad.

we know you have no money, but some other people have less.

The best thing is we're happy, with that we are truly blessed

we know there's not much for dinner but we're sure to have lots of fun.

we'll even light a candle and put it in the sticky bun.'

What the children said was too much for the parents to bear

and went to their bed with a tear, a thought and a prayer.

If there's some one out there listening were the words they heard say

don't let our lovely children have a miserable Christmas day.

Morning came, it was Christmas Eve when they heard the postman call.

Mum went down to see what it was and saw a letter on the floor.

She picked it up slowly thinking it was another nasty bill,

and opened it even slower expecting no Christmas thrill

But what she saw inside it made her nearly fall on the floor

For inside the envelope was a cheque for three hundred pounds and more.

She called to her husband and down the stairs he crept,

they both read the letter then wept and wept and wept.

For the taxman had got a bit generous that year although it was a bit late,

they had found they had over taxed them and gave them a tax rebate!

They then gave thanks to who ever it might have been,

who had listened to their prayer last night, and made their faces gleam.

When they pulled themselves together they thought what they must do,

quickly got the Christmas list out and down to the shops they flew.

The children did not know, what happened on that Christmas Eve.

They did not know the pleasure, their mum and dad had received.

The children on Christmas morning thought to give mum and dad a surprise.

They thought to give them a cuppa to show that love was alive.

Now the children did not know that while they were fast asleep

That Santa had made a call that night and in the house did creep.

The children crept down stairs to make a nice cup of tea

and the sight that was before them, made them scream and shout with glee.

For there in the corner was a great big Christmas tree all dressed up with light

and under it's branches all wrapped up and new were lots of nice presents and things to bite.


The children have grown up now and gone on their different ways and the parents have grown old and have gone a little bit grey.

But they will always remember that Christmas all happy and full of fun,

and they will never forget the offer of the candle in the sticky bun.

# The Cottage

It was back in 1982 that I first set eyes on the cottage. We were not looking for one to buy. Well not a thatched cottage, that's for sure.

It was more of a chance. We had sold our house, much faster than we had expected. It was in fact on the market for just two days. So we were left in a situation where we had to look around quickly, to see what was out there.

So we trudged all over the area that where we had decided to live. We found a few that looked interesting. As a matter of fact there was one particular house in Rowland's Castle that took our fancy. So we decided to go to the estate agent concerned, to find out more about the property. It was while we were in his office, that we noticed the cottage being advertised in the window. It looked interesting. So while it was a nice sunny day and not knowing what we were letting ourselves in for we went in and asked for the particulars.

The agent seemed to be more than willing and was only too pleased to take us to see the cottage that very afternoon.

As we approached the Cottage, we noticed it was completely surrounded by trees and overgrown hedge. When we drove into the drive what greeted us was a complete shambles, The drive looked more like a farm track, and the cottage itself was all broken down and looking more to be pulled down than to be lived in. All this we saw from inside the car. It was then that I said to my wife.

"Shall we bother?"

But she seemed to be quite intrigued by it all and wanted to go and look further. We slowly got out of the car and just stood for a moment or two just staring. If only to prepare ourselves, for what we were about to see.

Then my eyes were caught by the state of the thatched roof. I tried to see more of it, but it was covered in all kinds of vegetation. There was moss, which looked more like grass, and ivy that had stretched like tentacles over the roof and growing out of the thatch its self.

The house was all bent and twisted like an old man who was full of arthritis and full of pain, and was waiting for his death to put him out of his misery. I almost felt sorry for it.

I said to Yvonne my wife.

"Do you still want to go in?"

"We're here," she replied. "So why not?"

The agent, who was standing close by us said.

"Would you like the keys, so you can look inside?"

I then said.

"Don't you want to go in and show us around?"

"No not this time. I'll let you go round and look by yourselves."

I looked at him for a moment trying to see in his face something that would give us a clue, to why he didn't want to go in. What I saw was, fright or something close to it, not a lot, but most definitely some kind of fear. He reminded me of a child, who had just seen his first horror movie.

I put any other thoughts out of my head, as he handed me the keys. He then said.

"You will find the front door is bolted from the inside. So you will have to use the door at the back of the house."

I took the keys from him, and as we approached the cottage I noticed he had put himself into his car as if he wanted to drive off in a hurry.

I followed his instructions. We went through into the back garden, which was like the front, all overgrown and bedraggled, although it did look as if it was at one time well looked after. I walked slowly through the garden and I felt as if the house was looking at us saying.

"Who are you? What do you want? Go away."

I had a little giggle at my thoughts. We got to the back door, which was quite small, forcing me to bend down to prevent me bumping my head on the oak beam that straddled across the frame. But before we went in, Yvonne noticed two very large flat stones that were over to the side of the cottage. So over she went to look closer at them.

She then called back to me saying.

"Bryan come over her."

So ignoring the back door I went and joined her.

She then said

"What do you think? It looks like a grave too me."

I agreed with her and said.

"I wonder why it's there. Do you think there somebody under it? I think we better leave it alone."

We moved with care away from it, making sure we did not walk on it.

I could see by the expression on Yvonne's face that she was deep in thought, as to what we had just seen.

Going in to the cottage the first thing we encountered, was the overpowering smell of stagnation making it feel as if the cottage had been closed up for the duration of its life. I say life, because I had that feeling that the house was most definitely alive. It was very dark inside as the windows had been covered up with corrugated iron sheets full of holes which allowed shafts of light to penetrate the room, giving it a haunted look.

We walked though a narrow hall and on into the sitting room and like the room we had just left the ceiling was very low, making me stoop while walking though it. We then looked at the floor, noticing it was as bent as the rest of the house. There was a stairwell in the corner of the room, and looking further we found there weren't any stairs, just a rickety old ladder that was full of woodworm that led up into the bedroom above.

I checked it out to see if it were safe by slowly climbing the ladder, then Yvonne followed me. We didn't stay in the room for very long because I had that feeling of being sick from the psychic atmosphere, and wanted to vomit, not from my mouth but from the whole of my body. The feeling became so strong I had to flee down into the garden to get some fresh air. I was standing in the garden for a few moments when my wife came down to see how I was.

"I'm feeling better." I said and we both agreed, that it was the smell that made me feel the way the way I did.

Whilst we were in the garden, Yvonne decided to have a look around. I myself chose to venture back inside. I wanted to go with Yvonne, but I also felt as if I was being pulled back into the cottage. I got to the door, hoping that as we had left the door open for a while the smell would have been less potent. I will admit the stench had got a bit more acceptable. My interest was then was directed to the fireplace, for I noticed that at one time it would have been much larger than it was. The owner had fitted in a horrible 1950's monstrosity. I know the cottage was battered and broken but to install such, to me was totally barbaric.

After that we looked into a few more horrors. I decided to go and have a look at a second flight of stairs that led off the room I was in, and, I assumed, up to the north bedrooms. But standing on the first part of the stairs made me think very carefully about going any further. For it immediately the tread I stood on collapsed and intern jammed my leg making me topple over on to the stairs and by doing so, I put my arm through another tread. This made me express my opinion about the structure out loud. Whilst sitting there a bit dazed for a moment, I inspected the wood and found it was totally full of woodworm, and to make matters worse there were signs of deathwatch beetle.

So I thought that's it, I'm not going any further, I've seen enough I then went to go and see Yvonne and tell her what I hade found. But as I got to my feet, I felt I had to go further up the stairs. Not because I wanted to it was because I felt for some reason, I had to. So following what ever it was, I continued on up the stairs. Not stepping on the centre of the stairs but to the sides and all the time keeping my eyes on where I was treading.

It was then when I stepped on to the last tread, that I had a shock. It was when I took my eyes away from the stairs, and looked to my front.  I saw standing in front of me a young woman dressed like a Puritan in a long grey gown with a white collar. She was looking as if she was glad to see me, for she had the most beautiful smile.  But I can assure you, I was not glad to see her. The surprise very nearly made me fall back down the stairs. I closed my eyes for a second or two and made an oath to my maker, not knowing what I was going to see when I opened them again.  When I finally found the courage to open my eyes she was gone.

I leant against the wall if only to stop my heart from racing out of my body. I managed to calm my self and blamed the experience on my imagination. I then went back down the stairs only to meet Yvonne coming in. I said to her.

"Do you feel there's something odd about this cottage?"

She replied by saying.

"Yes I do."

Then I went on to tell her what I had just seen, and felt whatever it was, was following me around. The funny thing is I didn't feel frightened in anyway.

In the following days, we carried on looking at other properties, but were unable to keep our thoughts off the cottage. It was as if it had decided to keep a tight grip on us.

So to trying to break away from us thinking about the cootage. We asked some friends if they would like to come with us and give us their true opinion about it all. Our friends agreed and came with us on the following Saturday.

The my next negative encounter with the cottage was one of my friends braining himself on the beam over the door, very nearly knocked him out, but after some cuddles from Valda his wife and Yvonne, and a bit of play acting that you get from football player, a few swear words, that I shall not put in this story we waited until he was ready and all went our different ways and explore the cottage.

After we had a good look round we all gathered in the middle room and had a good natter about what we had seen, except Valda. She had remained silent and looked, deep in thought all through the conversation. It was her husband that mentioned it, by offering her a penny for her thoughts.  She remained quiet until she, with out changing her expression said.

"Bryan, when you came here before. Did you see anything or any one?"

My wife and I looked at each other, knowing what she was about to say.

"Why, Velda?" I asked.

"Well." She replied. "I've just see a young woman dressed in grey like that of a puritan."

Again, Yvonne and I looked at each other. I then said.

"Yes Velda. I did."

Of course my answer immediately put the wind up everyone. No answer or questions came. So we left it at that, for a while. We looked further into the bedroom and the large flat stone. On our way home we spent the time talking about the mysterious figure in grey.

We started work on the cottage almost as soon as we moved in. Yes we did buy the place. And yes we wondered if we had gone completely mad. Even until this day. We had to live in a caravan for a while until the winter drove us inside It wasn't much better apart from being able to light a fire. But the cottage was so draughty; we had to huddle around the fire to keep warm.

It took us about six months to clear all the bodge jobs that the previous owner had defiled the cottage with, which I might add included the draught holes. It was about then that strange things started to happen. We knew we were not alone and were being watched, but took little notice of it. Until we noticed the water taps were being turned on full. Then we found the electrical appliances were being interfered with. We tried to ignore it when we found that drawers were being pulled out and the clothing being spread across the bedroom. Incidentally the room was where we had seen the lady in grey.

We tended as we had so much work to do to put most of the happenings to one side.

It was not until we employed an odd job man named Clive that the real problems started.

We had done most of the work until we came to the fireplace in the sitting room. I had managed to handle the big timbers that surrounded it but found the brickwork needed a bit more than I could handle so hence Clive. The day he arrived, Yvonne and I had other pressing work to be done elsewhere. We fixed our builder friend up with tea coffee and instructions, in that order and left him by himself in the cottage.

That was our first mistake. When we both returned later that day we found the front door wide open. We called out for Clive, but there was no reply. We then walked into the sitting room. There wasn't a sign of him. Then looking to the floor we found a pile of cement, not used. Then his trowel, that was over the other side of the room, little bits of cement all over the floor and his hawk over near the stairs well. It almost looked as if there had been a fight.

Clive lived in a houseboat and had no phone so I went down to see him and find out why he had left, in so much of a hurry. Although I began to wonder at that time if he had met our resident guest. My thoughts were right. For as soon as he told me what had happened to him. I could understand why he had fled the cottage.

He said. "I'm not working in that place any more. Not for all the tea in china, well not on my own that's for sure. It all started about thirty minutes after you left; I'd just finished my cup of tea and started work on the fireplace, when a brick came down the chimney just missing me. I looked up to see where it came from but I couldn't see too much, so I carried on. Then I heard this noise coming from upstairs, which sounded like someone with heavy boots on walking across the floor. I stepped out of the fireplace and called out, to see if there was anybody there. There wasn't an answer. Then as I stood there, my trowel was snatched out of my hand and thrown across the room. The next thing so was my hawk. That went hurtling across the room as well. Then I heard them footsteps again. That was it I thought and left the cottage as fast as I could. I know it sound a bit daft, but that's what happened. I'm sorry I left the door open."

I tried to reassure him, but there was no shifting him. In the end I had to agree, that if he worked there again we must be there, and if we should go out anywhere. He would come with us.

By now it was getting late and it would be no use me asking him to come back right then.

I said. "We will be there all day tomorrow, if you should want to come along."

I then said my goodbyes and went home, all the time thinking what we must do about the problem. When I got home my wife, my son and I sat down over a cup of tea and talked about what had happened to the odd job man. We didn't mind the goings on ourselves, but felt something had to be done.

My first action, at the time, was to go into the centre of the house and try and reason with the spirits. I'd say to them, because I knew the lady I saw didn't wear hobnail boots. We all knew they were hobnail, because we had heard them ourselves. So I knew there was more than one ghost.

I said to them, "would you please stop messing us about. I know you're there, and we don't mind. But if it continues I will have to get someone in to stop you."

I thought that they might be trying to attract our attention, maybe getting fed up with us being here. But unfortunately after a few days they started again.

So I said. "That's it; I'm going to get the heavies in."

After that it did go quiet for a while. But I decided to go ahead with my threat. A few days later I contacted some friends that belonged to a mysterious group, called the Kabalah. What I'd heard about what the group did, they seemed just what I needed.

I told Jeff about what was happening, and asked him if he would come down and find out what is going on. He agreed, then came down the following Friday.

He brought with him, what he called his dogs. Who were two very psychic ladies who immediately, as Jeff said "had a sniff about the house"

It was not long before they returned back to the sitting room with the most bizarre story. This is what they came up with.

There are four of them in your house, one as you all ready know was a girl who's name is Sarah. She was living in this cottage some two hundred years ago. The family she belong to where Quakers who were very strict. Unfortunately for Sarah she became pregnant out of wedlock, which would have been a great shame on the family, so to hide her from public gaze; the parents put her in a smoke room until the child was born.

When Sarah finally gave birth to the child, the father snatched it from its mother and threw it on to the fire, to burn the Devil out.

The second, being the girl's father who is trapped here because of his deed. There was an older lady who was, in her life, an herbalist who gave her opinion during the service. That Jeff and his friends was a bunch of amateurs. We did find out later that she lived in a dwelling that was to the back of the cottage and was accused of being a witch. It was because of that. Her house was burned down and she along with her animals were killed.

After hearing all this we decided to arrange a service the coming weekend, as the group thought the matter was urgent. On the evening they were due to arrive. I thought to place a bell book and candle just inside the fireplace. I thought that it was the right thing to do. But as I placed the large Victorian bible on a stand, the pages started to turn by themselves. I was a little bit surprised, then put it down to a draught coming down the chimney and left it as that.

When they arrived and saw it. They had a little laugh, thinking it was a bit over the top. Then Jeff decided to look closer at the bible, and found to his surprise, that the page that it had turned to was the consecration service of King Solomon's temple. He then showed me his book of the service, and to my disbelief. There in front of me was the part of the same service he was to conduct.

Four people turned up that evening; I did not expect them all, as the weather that day was very wet and windy. All together there were nine in number. That apparently, according to Jeff, was the required number for the service. Jeff and his dogs then put on robes that resembled that of clergy. They then placed a sword and a staff on the small table I had put there for that purpose. They asked for the lights to be dimmed and then said "we will begin."

Then no sooner had they started, there was a blinding flash of lightning followed a large thunder clap which made us jump out of our skins and it was quickly followed by more lightning, that illuminated the room to such an extent, it put black shadows over my eyes, like that of looking into the sun. The thunderstorm then went on to increase in intensity as our friend continued the service.

Jeff raised his staff. I did not hear all he said as the storm was drowning what he was saying. I was hanging on to the low beams that were above me. It felt like all the energy was being drained out if my body. It was then that I saw the young lady appear over by the stairs behind my wife then superimposed her self over her. I tried to move but it was as if I was glued to the floor. I tried again.

Then Jeff said. "Don't worry Bryan, I know she's there."

There was another loud clap of thunder. That seemed to trigger off a dull blue light appearing on the table. All that were watching were completely struck dumb by what they were witnessing. Jeff raised the large sword that was before him.

He then shouted "Be gone. It is time for you to go to the place that is waiting for you."

The young woman that was Sarah then vanished along with the light that was on the table. He then gently laid the sword on to the table. Saying softly "it is done"

Jeff along with his dogs raised their arms and spoke in a language, which I did not understand. Then there was silence. For not only did our friends not speak, the storm had also stopped. The silence continued for a while, only to be broken by Jeff saying. "I hope it didn't frighten you too much."

Some of the guests, still remaining quiet, sat down. I did noticed that the house felt as if it had been cleaned and refreshed. I then along with my son looked out the window and found the sky was completely clear. Apart from a lone twinkling light that moved, going upwards, and out of sight

I can tell you all, that although it was like something out of a Dennis Wheatley novel. It did make me feel special to have been an instrument of what I had witnessed. You will draw your own conclusion to what I have told you.

But now let me tell you my conclusion.

After a few months had gone by, my wife and I decided to do our own research after being visited by two history students who wanted to know if there was a grave in our garden. We said there was something that looked like it might have been. They then went on to say that the grave was that of a young woman and her child, the young woman's name was Sarah Rogers. After talking to them for a short while and letting them see the stones. They went on their way. After that meeting we went around Hayling Island to find more information. We came across an old brick maker named Pycroft, who, after we had mentioned Sarah Rogers name told us more about her.

"Yes well "he said, "I know of her and I know she was at one time buried in the garden of your cottage. But later on, an old aunt had her remains and along with a child moved into St. Peters Church in North Hayling. After thanking him we went to the graveyard of the church. We did find a few Rogers among the graves but not Sarah's. So we went back to Mr. Pycroft and told him we could not find her in the graveyard.

He said. "No, no, no. I said in the church. There'll be a plaque on the wall with her name on it."

We thanked him again and ventured back over to the church. We went inside, had a look around and sure enough there it was right where he said it would be. It read, as I remember. Here lies the remains of Sarah Rogers and her child. We were so glad we had found her.

The old lady. We did find on an old map that showed that there was indeed a cottage there. The cottage was destroyed, along with an old lady, a very long time ago by fire. By the way, the old lady was banned by Jeff and co. from ever entering the cottage again as she caused too much trouble.

The father of Sarah Rogers was we think redeemed, because he was from the time of the service, no longer there.

As for the hob nailed boots, they are still walking the floors. Well they were when we moved. The house still creaked and groaned even though we had given it a new life.

Some things are never satisfied.

# Works by Frank Holt

## The Leather Armchair

We all lived above the pub called 'The Wheelbarrow' in Kent Road, Southsea. Our living quarters were on the third floor. The rooms were always well lit because our accommodation was nearly into the sky, into the clouds or bright sunshine.

My Mother and Father were working in the pub on the ground floor during the day, so they kept a dog for the extra security in the living rooms. Our latest dog a boxer was called Bonnie. He was always left upstairs on his own, supposedly to guard all of the rooms. When I came home from boarding school during the holidays I always ran up the stairs, so Bonnie would hear me. He would be walking around the rooms whenever I reached the top stair. But, but, but, sometimes, I crept up the stairs to see if there was a change in Bonnie's reactions. I went into the dining room where the leather armchair was, and there was poor old Bonnie fast asleep, and not doing his job. When I got near to the armchair those soulful eyes opened, and he knew he had been sleeping on guard duty.

My Dad used to take Bonnie over the common every day for his recreation, but Bonnie had a habit of running up to people and jumping up just like a boxer in the ring. He had a particular liking for the little children running over the Common. Unfortunately one time the mother of a child threatened my Dad that if it happened again she would go to the police and report the matter. So Bonnie was given away to a family living in Portchester, where they could spend time playing with Bonnie, all day.

On the first day of my holidays, after the loss of Bonnie, I was upstairs on my own and I decided to get a chair, put my feet up and quietly sit down in the leather armchair. You've guessed it I fell asleep. After an hour had passed I woke up, so from then on, I always believed the chair had magical powers, and that whenever one sat in it they fell asleep, soon afterwards.

I joined the Navy when I was older, and was sent to a minesweeper flotilla in the Mediterranean, to clear mines from the Greek Islands. My job was to guard the gangway and stop people getting onto the ship who were not entitled to do so. The ship was always moored to buoys in Malta, known as Sliema Creek. I was working the midnight to 4 o'clock shift. The fleet were warned that on the previous week the duty guard boat had come round to one of the ships at 2pm. The duty patrol officer had walked up the gangway when no one was about. He took the ship's log back to Naval Head Quarters. Of course after this heavy penalties were given out to the security party on that ship.

The minesweeper flotilla was composed of four ships, a very close knit group. When the end minesweeper got wind of the duty guard boat approaching, he would telephone the next nearest minesweeper and so on until all the ships were ready to wave at the guard boat, as it passed.

It was always quite funny to hear the telephones ringing all around the other ships. Naval Head Quarters always assumed that the minesweepers were on their toes because they were always looking for the odd rogue mines passing the Sweepers. But we knew differently?

One night I was patrolling the ship's fo'castle when I came across the Chief Bosun lowering a five gallon drum of paint over the side to a Maltese Dghaisas (Dyso) owner.

He said to me, 'Everything is alright here; nothing for you to worry about, you carry on.'

Not much I thought! I must enter this into my bank of favours for the future.

The Captain had his sea cabin near the fo'castle so he had one of his leather armchairs put on the front of the ship, so he could sit and have a few minutes peace after his dinner. Actually it was quite pleasant up there. To keep the sun off in the daytime, he had an awning covering the whole of the fo'castle. So consequently it was a good way for the Captain to view the other flotilla ships on the quiet known as on the (QT).

I was covering the eight to midnight shifts one night, and my duty was to keep guard on the fo'castle. I was surprised to see this leather armchair stuck at the point of the ship.

117

I circled it many times thinking no! I mustn't sit in it, but as the ship settled down for the night and everyone started to get their hammocks out, it got quieter and quieter.

I thought, well, who's going to know, just a little sit down, it's certainly a wonderful viewing spot from there, as the Captain had already discovered for himself. I weakened and relented, as I gingerly sat on the edge of the comfortable leather armchair. Mind you only on the edge, no sitting back. The next thing that happened was that I had a sixth sense after closing my eyes, someone else was approaching the fo'castle, I quickly jumped up and turned round. And yes it was our own Duty Officer doing his nightly rounds accompanied by the Chief Bosun.

The Officer said, 'Chief I think he was asleep, don't you?'

The Chief quick as a flash realised that he was accusing a man who had witnessed him selling paint and said, 'No, No, I'm positive he wasn't Sir.'

The Officer said 'Oh very well then. Keep a firm lookout.'

They both then went off to search some other parts of the ship. I was really disappointed with this little escapade because, it meant I had used up one of my little favours, all because of the magical properties of yet another leather armchair.

For recreation we were allowed to stay in an old RAF camp called Krendi. I spent six weeks there in total. They had a games room, and a shop selling cream cakes, cigarettes, and sweets. Not that many of us, purchased cigarettes as ours were always duty-free (6d.for 20).

A long time afterwards at home, I often looked at a Maltese street map to see if the camp was shown on it. Every time I looked for the Krendi Camp on the map, I could never find it.

Then one evening, years later, while settled in my own comfy armchair I started to read a new book called 'The Information Officer' the story being, about the days during the war in 1942 on the island of Malta…of course I wasn't there then, far too early for me. The story commenced with these so called 'Escorts' that kept on getting murdered as they plied their trade down the well known Gut in Valetta Malta.

I was very interested to find out if the writer Mark Mills ever mentioned Krendi in the book. My chair may have magical properties after all because it helped me solve the mystery of Krenda. On Page 42 he says,

"It was clear that the airfields had been singled out for the German bombing. Ta'Qali, Luqa, Hal Far, and the newer air-strips at Safi and Qrendi."

So no Krendi there then. I leaned back in my chair and the answer came to me. Wait a minute I do believe Mills is spelling Krendi with a Q. After all this time I have been thinking it was never a place at all, and all the time I've been spelling it wrongly. My new purchase of a Maltese map shows quite clearly Qrendi with the Q. Not only that but it has a history and an oddity.

To the south of the village there is a natural wonder known as Il-Maqluba, a huge hole in soft limestone some 100 metres (330 feet) across and 50 metres (165 feet) deep. The legend says, the inhabitants were so ungodly, with their filthy habits, that they, and their village were cast into hell, via Il-Maqluba, but even the devil rejected them, so they were all cast into the sea which formed an island, called Isle of Filfla, or filthy.

If I hadn't known the actual truth, it could have been the people of Malta trying to hide Qrendi from its very existence, and it's unreligious past history. Malta was always a strong Roman Catholic country, so if the people ever won anything, they were expected to give a proportion of their winnings to the church.

Another legend in Malta was if the newly married couples hadn't produced a baby within a year, the local priest would hang his hat on their door, stopping the husband from entering. Low and behold a new baby came into the family nine months later. But I, a non catholic and a man of the world can now spend my time in my own chair and wonder, no husband allowed and a baby in nine months, perks of the job?

# Gambit Queen

Frank had just gone into the Inspector's room.

'We've got a paedophile suspect down stairs and no clues. What do you suggest Sergeant?' The Inspector asked.

'You're not going to like this Gov but I want you to put someone else on the case, or bring in the special branch that deals with paedophile juvenile cases like this. What I'm trying to say is I would get far too emotional dealing with this case. I've a son of my own, so I'd become too closely involved.'

'Well this is a first…Frank refuse a case! Permission not granted, and for your information I want you to treat this one like a chess game. You're always telling me that's how to treat cases. So I know if you treat it like chess, you'll be so immersed in the theory, you'll forget all about your personal feelings,' the inspector said.

Frank thought, and then said, 'Perhaps you're right. I've never resigned in a chess game so I'll take your advice and interview the suspect. Thank you for the faith you have in me, to start this one…'

The Inspector interrupted, 'good luck and let me know how you get on straight afterwards.'


Frank left the office determined to solve the case quickly, forcing himself to ignore the distaste he felt. He got hold of Maisie, the duty constable arm and said quietly, 'I'm about to interview a suspected paedophile. How do you feel about that?'

'Actually Sargee I only recently went out on patrol making sure the children in the school playground were secure from sexual deviants. We spoke to one in the interview room; I found it very interesting indeed,' Maisie said as they both walked into the reception area.

'Good morning James, I'm Frank and this is Constable Maisie. We'd like to have a little chat to go over your statement, so if you'll step this way into the interview room,' Frank said opening the door for James and then he added, 'may I call you James?'

'Well if this is informal, perhaps you should call me Mr James.' He said taking his seat and giving an effeminate chuckle.

'I don't see the difference as your name is both James James there doesn't seem much point, and this interview is definitely informal,' Frank said taking his seat opposite, 'now start when you're ready James.'

'Well as I said before I prefer Mister James, if you'll please,' James said giving another chuckle and brushing his hair behind his ear.

Frank was up on his feet in a moment, and shouted at James, 'so you think this is a big joke! Well I don't! We are talking about someone's lost son.' Frank stormed out of the interview room with Maisie following closely behind.

'I don't fucking care Maisie, these bloody queers are all the same.' Frank said. After taking a long deep breath he added, 'I apologise for swearing to you just now, one thing I hate is men swearing in front young ladies.'

Maisie said in a quiet voice, 'I understand Sargee. I'll get James a cup of tea and a cream cake, that'll keep him quiet.'

'Why not a cream puff or cream poof, that should soften James up?' Frank said and laughed when he saw Maisie smile. Maisie gave a sigh and then went back into the interview room, thinking to herself that the Sergeant was in a better mood now. She hated seeing him in that bitter angry way. Losing it like that isn't very good when interviewing these tricky so and so's, as they played on situations like this.

Meanwhile Frank had time to get his emotions under control; he thought on reflection he would use a different tack. Leaning back in his chair his mind went over all the different chess moves and finished on the Gambit. This puts people off in chess who are expecting a different move. He went back into the interview as if the incident had never happened.

'Now where were we, Mr James? You're going to assist us in our enquiries, carry on were you left off.'

Frank knew at once he had made the right move; he sat back and waited for James.

'Well I heard you were looking for this little boy's attacker, and I wondered if I might help in your search. This man Roger in the local centre got to talking to me the other night about how he made love to a boy in the woods, and things got out of hand. He started to call out, so he put his hand on his mouth to shut him up, and it appeared he pressed far too hard. The boy went limp so he hid him in the woods amongst some willow trees that he previously slept in, it was in his homemade den.' James said.

Amazing thought Frank word perfect from his first statement. 'Made love! Don't you mean he raped him?'

'We don't call it rape, it's always love in our language.' James said.

'Is that so even when the other party is a little boy? Where can we find this Roger?' Frank asked.

'I only met him the one night and I've never seen him since.' James said.

'Well what did he look like? What kind of clothes did he have on?' Maisie asked.

James smiled and said 'Oh I don't remember things like that. It's always just talk anyway so I didn't take much notice when these blokes rattle on in the night. But Frank I was thinking that maybe if I help you, maybe I could get you off the sex offenders list in return.'

Frank stood up when his back was turned to James gave Maisie a wink. 'Why of course Mr James. I'll speak to the Inspector about the case after you give us more information. But at the moment you've not really given us anything except this man name called Roger.'

'Actually I do know a lot more,' James said 'I know where the body is hidden and the locality where it's situated.'

'That's excellent Mr James I'll arrange a car for us to go to the site and we can look for the little boy. I'll need to put hand cuffs on you, just a precautionary measure, and then you'll be entitled to our protection, alright with you Mr James?'

'Yes that's fine, you won't forget about our little arrangement will you?' James asked.

'As I said just now, I'll speak to the Inspector about this case. I feel sure some solution will be agreed on. Maisie will stay with you for the time being while I arrange for our little outing,' Frank said leaving the interview room to go upstairs to the Inspector, and to fill him in on the details.

The Inspector looked worried, 'all you've got Frank is the chance of a body and this unknown Roger. What are you going to do about him?'

Frank smiled. The Inspector had asked him to treat the case like a game of chess, Frank I would never tell someone what his next move would be. 'I've got all I want, and I know where to find our man Roger.'

'I'll leave it with you Frank I said you could solve this case easily,' The Inspector said, as he watched Frank walk out off the door.


They left in two squad cars to reconnoitre the sight as guided by Mr James and finally arrived at a field that James indicated.

'If you go over the gate – stile to a small wood of willow trees you'll find the body hidden in a make – shift den in the middle of the woods,' James said pointing.

When they got to the edge of the trees, James hung back on the outskirts, 'I can't go any further. I'm afraid of ghosts.'

Frank looked at James and hid the contempt he felt 'I'll need you to show us exactly where the body is. Why are you afraid of ghosts?'

He watched James become more agitated. His whole body started to shake with fear. 'I knew when I killed him he would come back to haunt me afterwards, but it was an accident.' He stopped himself and added, 'that's what Roger said to me.'

Frank had recognised the signs in the interview room. He had worked on another murder, and in this previous case the suspect was a schizophrenic who had really believed that it was the other person who had committed the murder. They get so confused they really believe it, like Doctor Jekyll and Mr Hyde Frank mused. James caught his attention by looking sheepish and brushing his hair behind his ear, 'I suppose our little deal is not on now.' He said a chuckle that gnawed at Frank's inside.

Frank immediately replied after hearing a constable shout, 'I've found him.'

'How right you are James. Maisie read him his rights and accompany James to the station.'

'It'll be a pleasure Sarge. It's a good job you had him hand cuffed.'

'Yes a lucky coincidence. Oh I forgot Maisie I don't believe in coincidences, see you over the Pub after you've locked James up. Oh I forgot Mr James, not for much longer though. He'll be getting a prison number instead of a name in the near future.'

Frank watched as his officers began to tape off the area, 'check mate' he said quietly.

# Germany's Downfall

Churchill switched on his intercom to his secretary in the next room; he heard the click of the phone as she picked it up.

'Yes Prime Minister, can I help you?'

'Peggy, get me the Commander of the Submarine Command in Scotland' Churchill said immediately.

'Straight away Prime Minister.'

After a few minutes the red phone rang, Churchill picked up the telephone and Peggy said,

'I'm putting you through now Sir.'

The phone crackled for moment and finally a voice said, 'Good morning Mr Churchill. How can I help you?'

There was always this banter between two people speaking to each other, the unwritten formality of speech, one using Mr the other using the christen name of the subordinate.

'Ah Gerry switch on your scrambler will you?'

'Switching on now Sir.'

'I need your best submarine and commanding captain on this one Gerry. Something very serious has come up, so I'm forewarning you now. I'm sending the Naval attaché with a car, he should reach you sometime this afternoon. Look after him Gerry, fix him up with some digs, he'll brief you on the details. He'll stay with you until the sub leaves Rosyth. I want him to report back to me afterwards.'

'Leave it to me Mr Churchill. Any details – what is this all about?' Gerry asked.

'No! All details will be in the diplomatic bag.' Churchill said and put the red telephone back on its cradle. Churchill sank into his large leather chair and thought we don't want any slip ups now; we're getting so close to the climax of this war, especially with Japan.

The attaché's car arrived at the naval dockyard and waiting by the gate was a Petty Officer, 'Good afternoon Sir, I'll take you to the Commander straight away.'

The Petty Officer waited for the attaché to get into the car, closed the door and then got in beside the driver and directed the car to the Commander's office in the centre of the dockyard. They made the short journey in silence. Once they arrived the Petty Officer escorted him to the office, knocked on the door, introduced the attaché and was quickly dismissed. As soon as the Commander was sure the officer had gone he got up from his desk and shook hand with the attaché Frank.

Frank settled into the chair, he knew the Commander desperately wanted to know what was going on,

'Bit of a flap this one, you'll need to keep this on a need to know basis, hence my delivering the instructions personally.'

He watched the Commander lick his lip nervously. Frank smiled and calmly put the brief case on the desk and took out the Naval Directive marked Top Secret.

'This document is to be read, but returned in my presence.' Frank said.

The Commander read the document carefully and handed it back and said, 'well I'm still confused. Is there any more you can tell me apart from the fact I have to give you my full co-operation and provide the best submarine and Captain in my flotilla of subs?'

Frank replied with a rue smile, ''fraid not but total security is essential and could cost us untold damage if any of this leaks out.'

'I do have someone in mind Sir, his name is Captain Stuart. And we've just overhauled H.M.S. Venturer so it should be fit for purpose.' Said the Commander

'Let me see this mans Stuart naval record. I will have to get him security clearance pretty pronto, like today. I'll get M15 to do it.'

The Commander produced Stuarts naval record from the drawer of his desk and handed it over. Frank was careful to hide his surprise and immediately suspicious. He didn't get to be Churchill's eyes and ears for nothing.

'I need to know how many people were involved in obtaining this document. Or did you, as I hope, get it yourself from the personnel filing cabinet.'

'When Mr Churchill said over the telephone his naval attaché was coming personally I got the file out myself.'

Frank studied the Commander and when he was satisfied that he was telling the truth he said,

'Good, good excellent news. Now when can I see Stuart privately?'

'I took the liberty of calling him here, he doesn't know why and is currently waiting in the visitors room downstairs.' The Commander said and glowed with pride when Frank nodded in approval. The Commander used the inter com and asked for Captain Stuart to be sent up. Frank took the opportunity to move his chair slightly so he could have a good look at the man. Captain Stuart gave an assertive knock and came in and saluted to the Commander. Frank observed a typical submarine man, he had a full beard and piercing blue eyes with a red sun tanned ruddy face. No doubt this comes from many hours standing in the conning tower guiding his ship through the high and low waves whilst charging up the batteries on the seas surface Frank reflected. But would he be the man for the job, the war had already claimed the lives of many great men. Still his first impression pleased Frank; he had a good handshake which he believed could tell you a lot about a man. Frank hoped that the rest of the investigation would go well.

'Nice to meet. Let's go to my car and we'll discuss some minor details Captain Stuart.' Frank said and seeing that the Commander was disappointed not to know what was going on added 'Thank you for your help Commander. My driver knows where I'm staying. I'll get him to telephone you from the hotel later to make further arrangements.'

As they got in to the car Frank said,

'What shall I call you, seeing as we might be working together?'

'Albert Sir, I hope I haven't let myself in for something that's a bit on the shady side?'

'Would that worry you Albert?' I thought a sub Captain would be more than willing to be involved in a little intrigue and variety.' Frank said carefully watching the Captain's reaction to his words.

'Well it's all this secrecy Sir. I like to prepare thoroughly before I go on a mission so as to iron out all the eventualities before they happen.'

Franks analytical mind began to work. He knew these studious people look and talk meekly but looks to be deceptive. He knew Albert could do the job demanded of him; he recently sank a German U – Boat. Who knows Frank thought, perhaps Albert like so many others fears me; knowing full well I can destroy anyone's career who dares to threaten my authority? Oh well he thought the meek shall inherit the earth!

'Have you ever tracked or followed another enemy sub without Asdic or managed to evade the enemy finding you under the sea?' Frank said putting his private thoughts away, he liked to start off any mission by asking a direct and involved question and seeing how, or if, any reaction was forth coming.

Franks ploy worked of course. Albert was very shocked at this line of questioning and for a moment felt like he was a student back at Dartmouth College. For an instant Albert was transported in his mind to a lesson were he had to get across a line of tables and chairs without touching the floor. But he hadn't become a Captain without being able to control his thoughts, he pondered the question and suddenly recalled that only the other day he had been talking in the wardrobe about using trigonometry for forecasting positions of the enemy by just listening to the propeller screws as they passed along in the sea.

Albert decided to see if he was correct and said,

'If Pythagoras and his Theorem could predict sides, heights and angles in the sixth century, I'm sure I can evade the enemy now.' Albert went on to explain his theory about listening to propeller screws.

'Excellent just what I wanted to hear, and how far away could you work out these enemy positions?'

They debated this theory until they arrived at the hotel. The driver opened the door so they could get out, as they entered the hotel reception Frank said,

'oh by the way Albert, your room is next to mine, and we will discuss the details further. If there's any thing you require just mention it to my driver, he'll purchase any toiletries or clothes that you need. We'll be together until this mission finishes. That's if you accept; of course if you don't it will be the secure block for you until it's all over. Lets hope all the checks are okay.'

The next morning Frank knocked on Albert's door to give him the news

'I'm pleased to tell you the jobs yours if you agree and sign the official secret act.'

Albert of course wanted to hear more about the mission and said,

'If it's for the country then I agree to accept your offer.'

'Good man after breakfast we'll drive out into the country and I'll explain everything there is to know.'

In the car Frank started to explain,

'The Germans are shipping something out to the Japanese via U-648, sailing from Pens of Norway so we'll have to head for the Baltic Sea and wait up until we hear from the Norwegian Underground, that the German U – boat has left port. Even this little part could be very costly to the Norwegians. We have reason to believe the Gestapo knows how important this escapade is and are monitoring everything around the area, including radio messages back and forward from us. Hence the absolute silence.'

'Might I enquire what they are shipping out?' Albert asked.

'You may unfortunately this will only be relayed to you when we are both on board the Venturer. Absolute silence no wives, friends or even messmates. I want a full load of torpedoes and anything you can suggest for the submarine. I take your advice on any calculating items or personnel – we could use a good torpedo operator. And don't bother about things like availability. Just give me the list I'll expedite.' Frank said then he added.

'I'm looking at some special sound equipment thought up by the boffins at Admiralty, you will come along and we'll decide if it's any good. We'll meet up again some time this afternoon.'

Frank and Albert arrived at the Rosyth gates as arranged; the Master at Arms met them at the gates and asked,

'What was all the flap about? There are two strangers waiting in the duty room with some special equipment.'

Frank said to Albert 'go along and sort out the meeting with the boffins, I want to discuss something with the Master.'

'Ah Master. Is there somewhere we can go and talk privately?' Frank said thinking to himself, pour chap he doesn't realise I'm at my most dangerous when I'm being polite.

The Master pushed out his chest like an over inflated self important cockerel and said

'We can go into my private room, if that's alright Sir?'

They walked into the Masters office and Frank calmly took the chair behind his desk. The Masters face showed his annoyance but he stood to attention at the other side of the desk.

Frank put clasped his hands together and leaned on the desk; he waited just long enough to make the man sweat and then said

'I understand Master that you have been asking questions about where the Venturer is going to and what's all the fuss about. For your information she is carrying out sea trails after her refit. Don't you like your post here in Rosyth? We have a listening post job at the Outer Hebrides for someone. He'll be away for about six months on his own up there. Would you be interested in the post Master? – oh and don't bother going to your Divisional Officer and complaining otherwise you both might end up in the Outer Hebrides. Do I make myself clear Master?'

'Ooo of course Sir – no problem at all – quite clear.' The Master mumbled.

'Good man I thought you would come round to my way of thinking after all we don't want to affect your long time good service or pension rights do we?'

Frank left the Master went on to meet up with Albert and the boffins.

'What do you think Albert, all sorted out?'

'We'll have to train up new sailors to work on the thing, also practise the equipment out on another friendly sub, but otherwise looks to me like a nice useful bit of kit.'

'That's settled then, the boffins will be coming with us, that suit you Albert? We'll all be leaving port tomorrow, as Nelson would say 'At High Tide'.' Frank said.

The submarine duly arrived from the Lerwick base in the Shetland Islands and they all went aboard after saluting the flag at the sub's stern.

The British code breakers at Bletchley Park (on the basis of Enigma decrypts, not for public knowledge) had learnt that the German U- boat U-846 was about to leave, and she was going South from Bergen. Frank called a meeting in the wardroom to discuss fully what the mission was going to be.

'Gentleman,' he said 'Adolf Hitler was very worried about how the war in Europe was going and he had a plan to get the Allies to send more troops to Japan. He was very impressed with the Kamikaze airplanes that continued to attack the American and British Carriers in the Pacific. But he realized how costly this method was to the Japanese. He also knew that the British Spitfires, although faster were fewer in number. Our planes have annihilated their German planes.'

Frank paused and filled his crystal cut glass tumbler with water from the jug on the table. As he sipped the water he could felt the tension in the room, especially the boffins as they were all civilians and didn't know much about underwater sea battles.

Frank continued 'He intends sending to Japan some advanced Messerschmitt Jet engine parts knowing full well that once they can produce these jet engines and get them into the skies they would hold supremacy in the air. No other country in the world has this kind of air technology. The Americans would have to divert valuable resources from Europe to Japan to counteract. We also have reports of a secondary cargo of 2000 canisters, this equals 65 tonnes of Mercury which was used in the production of weapons. He is sending this all by U boat to Japan.'

He paused again after explaining the reason this mission was so crucial. The men were anxious; they knew that failure would mean an early grave.

'Getting this information to us has cost the Norwegians dearly, in fact some of the mothers who had sons in the Resistance are past child bearing age, so you can emphasise they high cost they have paid. The SS started to round up lots of the known Norwegian Resistance fighters. They were shot against the towns centre wall. I trust you can now understand my anxiety in keeping this all a close secret. I have not and will not tolerate any person asking questions.

'Second important point our submarine carries 4 torpedoes and the U – boat carries 22 torpedoes. Probably not as many now with their secret cargo, but this needs to be considered. We need to get up steam and proceed to sea, to locate this U – boat, seek, intercept and destroy it.'

Frank looked at the men, and felt the weight of responsibly that only comes when one is forced to make life and death decisions on a daily basis and then said

'If there are no questions I wish you all success on our mission and I know you will all do your duty as professional sailors.'

He knew straight away that the men wouldn't question his authority they were career sailors. Once all the equipment and torpedoes had been neatly stowed aboard the submarine, the batteries recharged, they gradually pulled away from Rosyth to the open sea.

The Venturer spotted the U-boat periscope having taken evasive action. The U-boat was waiting for its escort. Albert waited 45 minutes before going to action stations and silent running. He was waiting for the U-boat to surface and thus present an easier target. Upon realizing they were being followed by the British submarine and that their escort had still not arrived, U-864 zigzagged underwater in attempted evasive manoeuvres. Each submarine occasionally risked raising their periscope to quickly see where each other was.

After three hours Albert decided to predict his opponents next move by using the new echo sounding device, he worked out that using the sounds he would be able to calculate the angle needed to intercept. Tension was very high amongst the men at this stage and nerves began to tingle at keeping the necessary silence. All of a sudden someone dropped a pen on the sub's deck. Everyone turned to the guilty party, it was easy to spot the culprit, and his face was a deep red colour. Frank kept his colour and slowly pulled his finger across his throats, denoting heads would roll if it happened again. The men instantly understood the unspoken message.

The first torpedo was released and then at 17 second intervals other were released. The other three torpedoes were set at different depths. Frank's assessment of Albert was correct. Anxiety spread over the men but Albert kept calm, he knew they would take 2 minutes to reach their target. A man at the helm glanced nervously at Frank but he wanted until the final charge was sent and then immediately gave the order to dive to evade retaliation from his opponent.

Unfortunately, the Captain of the U-864 was not as cool headed as the crew of the English submarine. They heard the torpedoes come and but steered into the path of the fourth torpedo, the U-864 exploded! It split into two and sank with all hands, it came to rest more than 152 metres below the seafloor. Albert got the bar to his DSO for his action. He never knew what reward Frank gained from his actions.

Albert did mention Frank to his wife after the war,

'I was very surprised that Frank the attaché came with us to see the whole task through, even in the submarine phase of the action. Any General in the army would be busy sticking coloured pins on his maps away from the real action, drinking brandy and discussing causalities.'

'That's why Mr Churchill chose Frank as the attaché not you.' His wife said.

'Actually darling Frank did say to me that anytime I wanted a spell in London in the Admiralty I was to just give his secretary a call.'

'Just think what fun I could have while you're at work visiting Harrods, Selfridges and going to Embassy Balls and Opera's.'

'I think I have had enough action my dear.' Albert said and his mind wandered back to the war.

He had made a very brave decision knowing full well that if he had missed they would have been defenceless against the U boat. He knew his calculations were based on solid figures and he was proud that a man like Frank had every confidence in him. But Albert had acted in the role has leader during the war and was happy to have that responsibility taken away now they were at peace. Unfortunately men of Frank's calibre with his unique way of thinking are always needed and Albert was never to know of the countless times Frank was to go on and save his country. Albert didn't even know that his use of the manual computation of a firing solution against a three dimensionally manoeuvring target was first used in his engagement with the U-864. Or that this method used by Albert and Frank became the basis for modern torpedo computer target systems. He did however refer to Frank has,

'Good old Frankie boy.' For the rest of his life.

# Jolson at Christmas Time

I was listening to the Managing Director of Marks and Spenser, Stuart Rose being interviewed by Kirsty Young on Desert Island Disks. She was certainly asking some tough questions. I wondered why it was that these people in Industry always answer some of her questions with such candour, when they are talking into the microphone rather than on television.

Stuart Rose started talking about his family, especially his younger sister when they were both living in Africa. He said that his sister's party piece was singing 'Mammy' in the style of Jolson. I can't ever remember a girl singing 'Mammy' except in the 1947 film 'The Jolson Story' when Evelyn Keyes was taking the mickey out of Jolson. He eventually married her in the film. This reminded me of my encounter with Jolson and the Mammy song.

Every Christmas just before closing time at The Wheelbarrow in Southsea, my Mum and Dad always held a Christmas Party. Dad used to go around the bars inviting some of his friendlier customers to stay behind for the Holt's Christmas party.

One of the games we played was called 'Sing, Say or Pay' so we all had an incentive to join in or pay up. I used to hate this game because my Dad was so versatile. He could play the accordion, ukulele, piano, electric piano, violin, drums etc, in fact you name it he could play it. The only song I could sing was 'Cherry Ripe' and I always thought it sounded sissy, but it was the only song in which I knew all the words.

So when the 'Jolson Story' was released I knew then I could sing the 'Mammy Song' in a good impersonation of the man himself. Years later I heard that Tom Jones and Rod Stewart were both heavily influenced by Al Jolson, in fact they both impersonated him on stage.

Later I joined the Navy and spent two years in the Mediterranean based at Alexandropoulos clearing mines that were left in the sea around the Greek Islands during the Second World War. Around Christmas time I was sent home to start a new course with two months holiday owing. I duly sent my mother a telegram stating 'Mammy I'm comin', I can remember it quite vividly because the telegraphist queried the spelling of Mammy, I said,

'The spelling is correct m-a-m-m-y.'

My Mum and Dad were married on Christmas Day. So they decided to have one big party to celebrate my home coming and there anniversary. My pal Ken and I went to a dance at the Embassy in Fawcett Road before the party started. When the dance finished we invited two girls to come back with us to the pub and the celebration party. They both ended up being sick so we sent them home in a taxi.

Now for the big surprise, we were all invited to the Sandringham Hotel where low and behold they had a microphone and band stand. We took Pat the pub's pianist with us and I was in my element. I sat my Mum down in the front near the piano, grabbed the microphone and sang 'My Mammy'. I knew that everyone at the party were very very surprised to see the quiet, shy, bashful Frank singing in front of his mother.

Afterwards someone filled up a pint glass with gin right to the top. I thinking it was water took a giant swig. Was I bad afterwards! But after being sick out in the back yard I managed to crawl back into the party, but I only drank water after that.

You may think that because I copied Jolson he was my favourite singer. You would be wrong. It was Al Martino singing 'Here in my Heart' or Mario Lanza 'Because you're Mine' a very big tenor singer in those days that I truly loved. Now it's Russell Watson. I suggested some titles he might like to sing on his second CD and low and behold when I bought the new CD the majority of the ones I'd suggested where on it. So now I imitate 'Catari! Catari!'

I can remember another party and the proprietor asked my Dad who was singing.

'Oh that's my son singing and you won't get him off the mike once he gets up.' My Dad replied.

The proprietor said, 'I think the song he's singing is 'Here in my Heart'. He's got style you should encourage time to take it up.'

'He don't want any encouraging.' My Dad said.

In fact some one associated with the Coliseum Theatre in Portsmouth also showed interest in me. But I didn't have any interest in a career where you wander around seeing the world and being paid for it at the same time.

I can remember David Whitfield managed to get a record contract whilst in the Navy. I always thought it was the Royal Navy because I tried to find out what ship he used to be on. When he died later in Australia they mentioned his time in the Merchant Navy. No wonder I was unable to speak to him, he was never in the Royal Navy.

It's a pity I didn't pursue my career in singing, perhaps I would now be sunning myself in the Bahamas with Cliff Richard. I wouldn't begrudge giving ten percent of my earnings to charity just like he did just to be famous.

Oh Happy Days! That have since passed us by.

# Telekinesis

The new girl was trim, petite and had red hair, and she understood accounts and bank reconciliations. I got her to check the company accounts and decided to make conversation.

'Did you see the television programme about that Russian, moving a china cup by telekinesis?'

'Yes. My husband and I tried to move vases around, but no success at the moment,' she said.

I replied, 'I had an out of body experience last week.'

Her wonderful brown eyes looked into mine and enquired, 'Did you go very far?'

Thinking given the chance, I might dear with you! I said 'No. I only got up to the bedroom ceiling and soon came down again.'

The next day when she came into work she said, 'I felt a presence last night and wondered if you had managed to transport yourself to our house?'

I wish, I mused.

'I'm afraid not,' I said with a twinkle in my eye and watched as she continued checking.

When I got home I was sitting on the toilet reading the paper as you do, reflecting on the red headed girl belief in telekinesis. I knew that I would have more of the mental aptitude than a red headed girl in accounts, when out of the corner of my eye I noticed a wood louse coming towards my feet. I quickly thought I'll try this telekinesis on it.

I said, 'turn back' waving my hand and asserting my will. And yes the wood louse immediately turned around and went back. Was it luck I asked myself? So I waved my hand left and with a clear command I said, 'go left.' The wood louse turned left.

I paused for a moment while I thought: problem, should I tell anyone of my discoveries? And while I debated what to do next I let the wood louse scuttle under the bathroom tile where it had come from.

# Works by Charlotte Comley

## Busted

I once had a dream that I was at meeting, and when I stood up I was completely naked. This was worse. I'd put on a few pounds, that's why I'd avoided buying new clothes. But nothing had prepared me for how I had felt trying to squeeze into last years dress. Of course, if I'd known my ex was going to be there I would have made more of an effort. But this last year with my nice, new cuddly, reliable boyfriend had made me lazy. I couldn't believe that I literally had nothing nice to wear. Then again we wore a uniform at the shop and if we did go out it was for a pub meal or a night at the cinema. So I held my breath and hoped no one would notice my gaping bust line. I was having quite a good time, and my new man was bringing us a second plate of sausage rolls when I stood up to pull down my jacket over my bum and there was Bill.

"Hello Jelly Belly," he crowed.

"Bill, I have asked you before, would you please stop calling me that," I said, looking at the expensive suit and tan.

I had to hand it to my ex – he certainly knew how to dress in style. When we had first met I couldn't believe my luck, how had some one so gorgeous picked me for a girlfriend. It wasn't until we married that I realised he spent more time in the bathroom than I did. We had been married four years when I realised that Bill couldn't stand any competition. He preferred to stand in the middle of a group of plain Jane's.

"Sorry Jenny. That's a lovely dress it would look prefect on someone thinner."

I smiled through clenched teeth and raised my champagne glass to my lips and waited for the next line. He liked to think himself a great wit. Bill didn't say anything else, instead his eyes darted round the room and he was clenching and unclenching his fists. A sure sign he was nervous but why?

"So how are you Bill? Business going well I see." I said nodding at his watch.

"Yeah great. You know me I could sell to anyone," he said.

But I wondered, was that smile forced? I was interested now. I usually tried not to think about my ex, but the absence of a long monologue about how many cars he had sold was very telling. I'd been worried about how the recession had been affecting the shop; of course it must be hitting the car trade harder. There it was again, his eyes darting around the room, they found their quarry and rested on a pretty blonde surrounded by men. She glanced over her shoulder and smiled at Bill, then pouted her lips and blew him a kiss. I couldn't believe the goofy look. Could my conceited, self absolved, narcissist ex husband be in love with some one other than himself? I waited for the jealously, it didn't come. I was definitely curious though, in a morbid way but not jealous. She sauntered over pausing to stop and smile at another man. I could feel Bill tense and enjoyed his discomfort. He positively gleamed when she finally came over. He slipped his arm around her waist and pulled her towards him.

"Jelly Belly er I mean Jenny I would like you to meet Kelly my fiancée," Bill said. The smug smile was back.

"Nice to meet you." I said and felt her eyes take in the buttons straining to make the fabric hold. She looked like a gazelle, slim, pretty and perfect. She was wearing one of our designer dresses, new season. I couldn't remember the exact price but it was well over £200. The way the fabric flowed in soft curves flattering her figure, it must have been exactly what the designer had in mind. I realised that Bill was talking.

"Her Daddy doesn't like her to work. He is old fashioned. I think I won him over with my charm" and with a smile added" and rugged good looks."

"Why would her father be bother about what you looked like?" I asked.

Kelly let out a little giggle and was about to say something when Bill cut in. He hadn't changed that much.

"No doubt that he knows how good looking the grand kids will be. Once he sees how well I look after the daughter. I know he'll want me to look after his business."

"Yes Daddy was excited about you being such a successful business man." Kelly said placing a little kiss on Bills cheek. "He told us all about his companies."

Bill threw me a glance. I was very tempted to point out that the car lot on the outside of town wasn't really what you would call 'companies'. It was my turn to smile at Bill.

"Yes when Bill talks about his – companies- it is very impressive," I said finishing my champagne. No doubt they will both end up in a big house, huge car on the drive and two beautiful skinny children to put in it. I sighed, just my luck. When I was married to him he wouldn't pay the rent for the flat but would blow a thousand pounds on a watch. Trust him to marry money. No wondered he was clamping on to her like a life jacket. I listened to them whittle on about money and thought about my little two bedroom house. My boyfriend came back with the plates piled high; I enjoyed the fact that he didn't give Kelly a second look.

"Sorry I was so long but they were bringing out the gateaux's and I know how much you like a bit of cake." He said.

Bill snorted with laughter, "you can say that again."

My boyfriend stiffen and looked down into Bill's eyes. I loved the fact that he was just so big and tall.

"Well we'd better get on and circulate." Bill said.

I sat down with my meaty man and listened to him describe the cheesecake. "You look really pretty today. I think I'd like to see you in a white dress" He said between mouthfuls and giving me a wink. I blushed at his understated proposal. I knew that I'd rather have a nice man than a rich one.

I was looking at the wedding dresses on the third floor when I saw Kelly. I had to dash back to the returns counter.

"Can I help you?" I asked. She doesn't recognise me I thought.

"Yes I'd like to return this dress. It doesn't fit properly. It still has the label on though." She said without making eye contact. She carefully pulled out the floral silk fabric with the rose pattern. I looked at the label and the tiny tell tale holes where she had pinned the label away from sight.

"Did you enjoy the wedding Kelly?" I asked.

She looked confused for a moment and then her eyes strayed down to my bulging bust and then realisation dawned. She carefully pushed the dress back in the bag.

142

"You won't tell Bill. Look, Daddy's had a few problems. If Bill knew he might think I was just marrying him for his money, and I'm not. I do... care for him."

"Don't worry, I won't say a word." I promised.

# Labels

I took off my ID badge that claimed I was a bank manager, picked up the volunteers' list of the Horticultural Show and popped 'Show Organiser' badge around my neck. This year as well as flowers, vegetables, stuffed scarecrows I had made the revolutionary decision to add jams and cake to the competition.

I placed my Victoria sandwich in the centre of the table, aware that it looked nicer than the lopsided offering of Mrs Peters. It took me only a few moments to rearrange the decorations to make the younger WI member's attempt at a display look more professional and stylish.

'Now that does look better?' My fellow judge said.

I knew that he coveted my role as chairman on the committee. Oh, I was aware of the resentment of the easy confidence of my smile, the gentle elegance of my manicured hands and the warmth in my voice. My children's long list of academic achievement and my husband's company car.

I won of course and accepted the blue ribbon. I had put newspaper in the boot before I set out to lay the thank you bouquet on. On arrival at home I carefully placed the judge's badge and show notes into my filing cabinet for next year. Once I put on my apron and the evening meal was simmering nicely I arranged my flowers and set the vase on the highly polished table. I met my husband by the door with a small kiss and drink then retreated to the bathroom to fix my make up before dinner. And there in the reflection underneath the foundation I saw my true self. A woman with too many responsibilities, too few resources, too little control, too little encouragement and no end in sight.

# Works by Toni Wood

## Herbert and Claire

He was relieved that it never changed, there was the frost and it was just beginning to become warmer, but he had stood at this window for ten winters and the frost and the snow has regularly settled. Herbert was glad that it stayed constant; the people in the other flats didn't. There had been students last Christmas, the constant noise and when he had asked them to turn the music down they has shrieked with laughter and turned it up.

The bell rang; he put the cat down, walked to the front door and opened it.

"Recorded delivery," said the postman.

Herbert always thought of her as a postman, but in fact she was a post woman. She was about forty. He was never sure of women, he had very little to do with them, only his mother and now she was dead, just like her to go a week before Christmas. It was almost as if she timed it, as she did with everything in her life, by the book, always calculated to avoid any risk of error. That's how she had loved her family – himself, his sister and their father, it has said in the motherhood book love and she had.

"Lovely morning," the post woman was always brisk, her appearance was short and square, Herbert disliked her perpetual attitude of optimism. He suspected she was happy with her life.

"Yes it is," He thought it was too cold "Frosty but sunny, that's how I like it." She was going to leave. He looked at the letter from the solicitor, details of his mother's last will and testimony no doubt. He would open it after breakfast.

"Will you be going to your sisters this Christmas?" she paused at the door. It made Herbert uncomfortable, her being so near.

"I don't know, I'm not really sure" he was surprised by the remark

The cat slithered through the door and smeared its face across her trouser leg. She bent down and caressed its face.

"What's her name?"

"Hilda."

146

"That's an odd name for a cat,"

"I thought you were talking about my sister."

"Well it doesn't really matter, either will do," she replied.

Herbert thought she was always so amenable.

"I just call her cat," he said.

"Oh, she should have a proper name."

"Well, I must be off, the morning is not yet over, the post needs delivering" she strode along the hall, down the stairs and opened the door. Herbert watched and resented the easy, but busy way that she approached any obstacle. He suspected that she enjoyed her life; he would try and avoid her from now on.

"Bye," she called as she opened the front door.

"Goodbye." He said. She did not hear him.

Herbert's Saturday continued with inevitable sameness, he had a little breakfast, fed the cat and then went through to the bedroom. This room was small and in the corner was a basin made of porcelain. He put the letter on the dressing table; he didn't what to read it just yet. Filling the sink he performed his ablutions with a practiced sweep. The bathroom was down two flights of stairs, shared by three other flats. The thought of washing where others had already made him feel slightly revolted. Consequently, he only took a bath once or twice a month. But he was scrupulously clean and when he had finished and looked in the mirror, his face was shining, hair neat and teeth brushed until they gleamed.

Taking the coat from behind the curtained wardrobe in the corner of the room, he pulled it on. The cat, back leg projected in the air, systematically cleaning its rear end, paused, then jumped off the bed. She knew he was going to the park and would follow; there she would desert him in her selfish manner. Accompanying him down the road ensured she would not be molested by the spiteful minded children who lived in the surrounding tenements and flats: they screamed with pleasure when they saw any living creature, dog, cat, butterflies, bugs and assorted mini-beasts, and would chance and victimise, and in the case of insects, crush with hysterical laughter anything that tried to flee in terror.

The park was busy that morning. He approached his usual bench. It was empty.

"Got your Christmas presents yet?" That voice was loud and caustic. Frightened him he turned and looked behind. The old tramp, a woman, limped toward him on a broken foot that had never been set properly. The rhythmic bob remind him of decaying seaweed adrift in the sea. He saw the crumpled pile of dirty newspaper under the bush. Herbert's hesitating was for too long! She was by his side in a moment; on occasions she went to the Salvation Armey centre and they had washing facilities that he guessed she used. She could not have been for some time, the smell nestled onto his clothes and made him retch.

"Go away;" he hissed

"Oh you don't mean that, I know you come here just to see me."

Herbert knew she was a liar, the time she had told him that there had been a robbery in the nearby jewellers shop and the police had been asking for witnesses, or for people in the park that day to come forward, he had gone to the police station but they had not known what he was talking about. She in turn had replied, 'April Fools!!' lying and cackling with pleasure. Herbert had said that she was a wicked depraved old hag and ought to be locked away. But they both knew that she often was and had spent short spells in the psychiatric hospital and the jail, he had also hoped she was due for a 'visit' soon, visits to the park would then be undisturbed.

"Well Mr Snooty," she rose from the bench and with a mock gesture of defence, hobbled off.

"Hey there, so this is where you slope off to then,"

Herbert looked up in surprise, he knew immediately that it was not the old tramp; he never had this amount of human contact in one day in such a long time, not since the times that his mother and sister had come and descended on him, organising his affairs, making him feel inferior and upsetting his otherwise peaceful existence.

He felt oddly excited about these two women, for he recognised the post woman's voice, wanting him. The post woman leaning over her bike and scooting it, stopped at the bench and put it firmly against the back. She lifted the bag off and pulled out the flask.

"Don't mind if I sit and have a cup of tea with you? Would you like one?" She was making herself comfy by his side.

"Ere, what you doin' wiv' im?" The old vagrant, half way across the park turned back, she hobbled fast and frightened the pigeons settled on the grass. Herbert watched in terror then quickly stood up, took the post woman's arm and led her in the direction of the caged birds, she almost dropped her flask and only just managed to grasp her bike and move off.

"So you got someone else, a?" The vagrant complained.

"Who on earth is that?" said the post woman.

She was puffing now, clouds of breath forced out and condensed in the air. Herbert puffed too and when he stopped at the cages to look for another bench, they looked at each other and smiled. Her short cropped hair, round solid face and light cheerful eyes made him grasp her arm and sit her on the bench. Feeling so impulsive annoyed him, he was accustomed to going at a slow and steady pace, with very little hurry, today was upsetting, touching this woman was upsetting.

Children were walking up and down in front of the caged birds, the post woman still grasping the bike, rose and secured it to the back of the bench. Walking over to the cage she took out a pack of sandwiches and helped a small boy push pieces of them through the wire.

"Darren don't you get your fingers pecked!" the woman next to Herbert shouted. Large and fat, face swollen with exertion, she bulged onto the seat and into Herbert's side. She threw the words out as an addition to her conversation about what Herbert guessed, was a broken washing machine.

"Then the bloke came again and the bloody thing split, wouldn't work at all so, will you look at that child, never does what he's told."Her companion, a thin woman with long lank hair and no teeth, submissive to the larger woman's onslaught of words, looked around and did not comment.

"Then the new washing machine came," she leapt up and swaying from side to side lumbered to the cage. The child, who had previously ignored her demands, was forcing his finger through the cage, started to run, but she caught him by the coat and hauled him back. The post woman, bent over the cage straightened and was about to protest but thought better of it. The large woman shook the child,

"Now ruddy well do as you're told!" she released him, he in turn returned to jamming his fingers through the wire mesh as soon as her back was turned and she had gone back to her seat.

"Herbert, come and feed the birds," the post woman called.

He got up and went over to the cages

"How did you know my name?" he asked her

"From your letters,""Mine is Claire"

A small girl was trying to put a piece of bread through the caged wire, he bent down and helped her. That was the first time he had been close to child. He was surprised that her hand was so soft. He drew away quickly.

"Don't be afraid, they don't bite", Claire said gently, children that is."

"I go to school soon." It was the little girl, looking up at them and smiling.

"Do you want to go?" Claire asked

The little girl did not answer; she skipped to the next cage and left them standing alone.

"Look at that one Herbert; it has plumes on its head."

In all the years that he had been coming to this park he had never looked in the bird cages or even bothered to distinguish one from the other.

"Would you like to come to the Christmas dinner at the Guildhall?"

"I don't know" he was shocked at the request. He had imagined that men should do the asking.

"You're full of indecision aren't you?" she smiled

"I'm just not accustomed to strange women asking me out."

"I'm not strange, I have been delivering your letters for the last four years and saying good morning for the past two. Not that you have ever replied with any urgency. You never bothered to look at me for the first year, and then when you finally did it was only to nod and grunt a dismissal."

It never occurred to him that someone actually wanted to be near him, he was shocked and ashamed at his behaviour.

Claire was smiling, her eyes laughing. He realised that she really did enjoyed life. Perhaps he could too.......

# The Mysterious Brown Paper Parcel

There was nothing else left to do but open the damned thing. It had been expected and received. Waiting on the table, it needing to be lifted opened and faced. But when would be the most opportune moment. Vivianne hoped the noise that it emitted would ceases, a gentle hum that encircled her ears and pleaded for ways out. How could something the colour of desert baked grass and so uninteresting, be responsible for such a degree of foreboding. She had hoped Michael would have arrived by now, calling him, an hour ago, immediately the parcel had been delivered, signed for and place on the table, Vivianne suspected that his presence could ensure a lessening of the cursed prediction?

She grabbed a clean freshly washed wine glass and threw open the fridge, Pinot Griso was best at a frighteningly frosty, low temperature, she poured an ample glass.

There was a gentle tap, Vivianne swung around, balancing bottle, glass and fridge door she manoeuvred the bottle back in. The doorbell chimed! Within several paces and a flick of the door catch she greeted Michael with a warm smile, leant forward caressed his neck and drew him across the threshold, into the small flat.

'When did it arrive?' the question was urgent, intending as an answer Michael slipped his hand around the back of her waist and drew Vivianne close. To approach the parcel united was reassuring.

'About an hour ago',

'Why doesn't it stop that wretched noise? When it is open, can we be sure that the curse will leave us in peace?

Vivienne knew he could not answer the questions, not with any great certainty, but to face the reality that lay within these spoken words gave her courage, particularly when facing along-side with

Michael. She had known him for many years, as a colleague, friend and lover.

For her he represented the strength and integrity that only truly great men possess, and at this precise moment in time, with the possibility that a force of evil, so great, mankind would face a catastrophic demise, she needed him. The wine drunk, the apartment door firmly closed and the parcel raised for a closer examination, Michael recalled the circumstances that had captured the contents. He knew the magnitude and responsibility of the task. He recalled the scenes of pain and carnage that the contents of this parcel had caused, watched then and recalled now, so long ago, and yet it only seemed like yesterday.

The thickly carpeted jungle floor, the dense impenetrable vegetation and the desperate need to find the hidden idol........once found the idol had held the code to unlocking the talisman.

Their journey to Paraguay had been long and difficult. The airline flight endless, food tasting of unsavory engine oil, 'engine oil....what do you mean engine oil' had been Michael's retort. He could not begin to fathom Viviennes's taste, particular her insistence concerning the finest food. His personal belief was that food was a necessity because it satisfied hunger; she viewed it as an art form in terms of the textures, colours and flavours, to be appreciated finely and consumed patiently. There had been no good choice of wine and this had prompted further her dissatisfaction of the catering, because there would be no accompaniment to her meal.

Vivienne had questioned the practicalities of Michael's insistence for keeping their costs low. But the lack of room to move about, the food, the fellow passengers, all who seemed to be a varied mixture of South American; speaking Spanish loudly, soothing or chastising their young vehemently, all in economy class, depressed Vivienne and by the time of their arrival at Rio de Janeiro her patience long fled, hot, hungry and accusing, Vivienne wanted only the cool peaceful sanctuary of their familiar hotel surroundings.

This being the couple's third visit, the staff knew and respected them both, they were quickly registered, assisted and ushered to their room.

Michael wasted no time in making contact with Professor McGuire, he would know where the talisman would be kept, it was to meet with the Professor that their next move would be.

But the meeting never occurred Michael had recalled the sense of fear and increased desperation as the days had passed and the calls, to Professor McGuire, three in total, were not returned.

There had been newsflashes, on the local Hispanic television channel, of how the professor's body had been found. He had been dragged from a well that the locals used for collecting their daily drinking water. There was an outcry, the well closed and the local Mayor's office stoned persistently, until he agreed to have the well cleaned and re-opened.

Vivienne and Michael had returned then, to Britain, no idol, no possible lead to where it might be traced and dispiritingly their one and only possible trace dead.

It was unnatural stain that had been left on the table, was the same stain that was smeared across their grotesquely positioned bodies. That was how Inspector Harris had found them, a distorted and fixed grimace upon each face! The man, tall, dark-haired named as  Michael Ellis, and the girl, attractive, mid thirties name of Vivianne Harcourt, locked in a terrifying close embrace…as if trying to save each other from whatever it was that came from the parcel and destroyed them both.

If he could just track down what it was that had made the brown strains, and what if anything had come from the parcel, he felt sure other clues to the victims death could then be deduced.

But the parcel had already traveled on further than Inspector Harris would ever have imagined........search out <u>his</u> place.

# Work by Melissa Collyer

## Love

When you love someone nothing can tear you apart
Time slows down, but the world keeps spinning
And you willingly give up your heart.

When you love someone your life seems perfect
Like nothing could ever go wrong,
You're automatically happy and never upset
And your life never seems to go down.

When you love someone you should be loved back
And cared for just the same,
It's no fun being sad
As it will just drive you insane!

When you love someone you should feel somehow different
Like your life is now complete,
That hole in your chest that needed filling,
Is filled with your loves heart beats.

When I love someone things never seem to go right
And soon pain and anger kicks in
At the fact that I don't seem to be right or to my love,
My feelings won't sink in.

However I know that one day I will be happy
And eventually I will find someone
As if your strong and just move on
Your broken heart will be one.

www.ingramcontent.com/pod-product-compliance
Lightning Source LLC
Chambersburg PA
CBHW071345170626
46811CB00003B/990